Autumn in Glenkeld,
Pumpkins & Firelight.

The Glenkeld Series

by Kara S. Lang

Kara S Mann

Autumn in Glenkeld: Pumpkins & Firelight
© 2025 Kara S. Lang

All rights reserved. No part of this publication may be reproduced, stored in a retrieval system, or transmitted in any form or by any means — electronic, mechanical, photocopying, recording, or otherwise — without the prior written permission of the publisher.

This is a work of fiction. Names, characters, places, and incidents are products of the author's imagination. Any resemblance to actual persons, living or dead, or actual events is purely coincidental.

Published by KDP imprint

For everyone who knows the joy of coorie nights —
may you always find warmth, pumpkins, and firelight.

Contents

Chapter 1 — Pumpkins and Firelight 6
Samantha's POV 6
Chapter 2 — Sawdust & Sunlight 18
Ethan's POV 18
Chapter 3 — The Pumpkin Patch 30
Samantha's POV 30
Chapter 4 — Golden Light, Sharp Edges 36
Ethan's POV 36
Chapter 5 — Lanterns & Small Confessions .. 45
Samantha's POV 45
Chapter 6 — Heat in the Grain 54
Ethan's POV 54
Chapter 7 — Embers & Edges 63
Samantha's POV 63
Chapter 8 — Stormglass 73
Ethan's POV 73
Chapter 9 — First Flame 83
Samantha's POV 83
Chapter 10 — Hearth fire 92
Ethan's POV 92
Chapter 11 — Morning Honey 101
Samantha's POV 101

Chapter 12 — Measure Twice 111
Ethan's POV... 111
Chapter 13 — Hairline Cracks 119
Samantha's POV... 119
Chapter 14 — Grainfire 129
Ethan's POV... 129
Chapter 15 — Bread & Fences....................................... 138
Samantha's POV... 138
Chapter 16 — Wild Weather, Kept Promises 148
Ethan's POV... 148
Chapter 17 — Honeyed Midnight 157
Samantha's POV... 157
Chapter 18 — Thunder in the Grain 164
Ethan's POV... 164
Chapter 19 — The Long Flame...................................... 172
Samantha's POV... 172
Chapter 20 — Ever After, Kept Warm 180
Ethan's POV... 180
♥ A Note from the Author.. 188
About the Series.. 190
About the Author.. 191

Chapter 1 — Pumpkins and Firelight
Samantha's POV

The bus leaves me in a gust of diesel and wet leaves, its taillights blinking away like a stubborn spell I've decided not to cast. I stand in the square with three suitcases, one battered laptop bag, and the kind of optimism that feels like a dare. Glenkeld is all slate roofs and whitewashed stone, bunting strung from lamppost to lamppost in a fluttering parade of russet and gold. Pumpkins perch on stoops as if waiting to be chosen. The air smells like woodsmoke, apples, and the sweet ache of cinnamon.

This is why I came. A small Scottish town tucked into the hills, where October seems to have moved in permanently and nobody minds. A fresh start after a relationship that ended so badly, I refer to it, uncharitably, as The Toad Incident. Not literally—no amphibians were harmed—but if my ex had sprouted a warty snout and hopped off toward a damp, contemplative life, I wouldn't have argued with the universe.

I trundle my suitcases up Rowan Lane, a narrow ribbon of cobbles with ivy-draped walls and fox-shaped door knockers that watch the world like mischievous sentries. Number 7 tilts companionably against its neighbour, blue door scuffed by years of Scottish weather, a wreath of wheat and eucalyptus hanging as if it knows it's photogenic. I fit the brass key into the lock. The latch gives with a sigh, and something in my chest exhales with it.

Inside smells faintly of soap and peat. Sunlight lays itself along the honeyed boards. There's a small sofa with a folded tartan throw, a round table that begs for tea and emails, shelves that promise to learn my favourite spines by heart. The kettle sits on the stove like a faithful dog. I curl my fingers under the windowsill—cool, solid—and let the room's quiet settle into me like a second sweater.

"Hello," I say to the house, because people don't have to be the only things greeted. "I won't make a mess. Much."

I unpack the necessary bits: laptop on the table, chargers tamed with a hair tie, a jar of pencils, my favourite mug with a chipped lip. When I hang my yellow raincoat by the door, the fox knocker catches the light and—this is ridiculous—winks—not literal—close enough. I blink back. "We're all behaving, yes?" The knocker, being metal, refuses to answer.

I make tea and pull back the curtain. Outside, the lane is a miniature opera: a kid steering a wheelbarrow piled with tiny gourds, a woman in a pom-pom hat coaxing a terrier past an offensively handsome tomcat, a man chalking up the café board with today's specials—Cullen Skink, Spiced Pumpkin Scones, Toffee Apple Latte. The chalk squeaks in a way that makes me think of school and brand-new starts. A fiddler a street over unspools a tune that sounds like home to someone; maybe it could be home to me if I let it.

I drink the tea. I fail to pretend I'm going to work. The town calls me the way an unwrapped present calls a child. Five minutes later, I'm out the door.

Glenkeld throws its arms wide and presses a kiss to both my cheeks. The square bustles: crates of apples with bloom still on their skin; jars of honey that glow like captured afternoons; a florist twisting twine around a bundle of branches that might, with the right candles, look like a spell. Paper lanterns—painted moons, ravens, and smirking pumpkin faces—bob overhead. Every shop window has put on its best October. The butcher's has a garland of dried orange slices. The post office displays knitted ghosts with button eyes. The bakery has sugar-dusted doughnuts arrayed like little halos.

I buy one. I shouldn't, but I do. It tastes like childhood and mischief. Cinnamon crunches, sugar dissolves, and I hum against it, ridiculous and happy. In that moment—powdered sugar on my lip, violin weaving through the air, a soft breeze lifting the hair at my nape—I feel the world tilt into a kinder orbit.

A bell chimes when I push open the bookshop door. The scent is dust and cardamom tea and ink. Shelves lean into each other like old friends. A ladder grazes the ceiling near the front window where sun slants in at a flattering angle. Bunting—tiny felt leaves in auburn and gold—drapes the window like a soft smile.

And on the ladder: a man.

He's tall even when he's above me, all line and substance, shoulders filling out a faded black Henley shirt, old denim dusted with sawdust that turns the sun into glitter. Dark hair does its own stubborn thing, as if a hat has never successfully tamed it. His hands are nicked and sure, tying the last loop of bunting with a care that makes me ache for no good reason. When he glances down, I realise his eyes are the exact grey of sea before a storm, and also the kind that remember what they've seen. His gaze flicks to my mouth and back—polite, unhelpful—and I swipe an imaginary trace of sugar away with my thumb.

"Ye've the look of a reader," he says, voice a low rumble that makes the ladder tick as if it agrees.

Ten possible replies pile up in my throat and fight to be first. The one that gets through is not clever. "I like books," I manage. "And bunting. And autumn. Not necessarily in that order."

One corner of his mouth lifts, not quite a smile, like he's unpractised at giving himself away. "D'you now."

"Ethan, darling, you'll have that door right in a jiff?" calls a woman from behind the counter. She's fifty-ish with a silver streak and thistle earrings; her name tag says Morag. She takes me in with a bright, appraising glance. "And you must be Samantha—No. 7 Rowan Lane, aye? I left you a loaf of brown in the bread bin yesterday, hope you don't mind. Welcome to Glenkeld."

I feel the oddest prickle of tears. "You left me bread?"

"It would be a crime to let a new lass arrive to bare cupboards," she says, decisive. "City folk forget that hunger makes fools of us all."

"I'm from everywhere," I say, which is true and also dodging. "Software engineer. Nomadic goblin. Will code for tea."

"Tea, we have." Morag nods at the back. "And books. And gossip. Ethan, come say hello properly."

The man on the ladder—Ethan—descends with unhurried precision, an economy of motion that suggests he wastes neither time nor words. On the ground, he's taller still, the shop suddenly a size too small for him. He wipes sawdust on his jeans, leaving pale streaks.

"You'll be the lass from America," he says. Not a question, exactly. More an assessment he's willing to update with new data.

"I'll be the lass from anywhere with Wi-Fi," I answer. "But yes. America, last I checked."

"Glenkeld's a good place to stop." His gaze skates over me like a hand checking a plank for splinters—gentle, assessing. "Muir Farm for pumpkins. Mind the geese."

My eyebrows lift. "This is the second time I've been warned about geese today."

"Right," he says gravely. "Then we've a chance of keepin' ye in one piece."

The bunting above him stirs though there's no breeze inside. A felt leaf brushes his shoulder and then the counter, landing near my hand. It's nothing. It's a draft. It's the kind of coincidence that pricks the skin like a static kiss. I clear my throat.

"Do you believe in magic?" I don't mean to ask it. It spills out anyway, impulsive and embarrassing.

Morag's smile brightens like a match. "Oh, don't." She fans herself with a flyer. "You'll have him tying charms to every door handle from here to the glen."

Ethan doesn't smile, precisely. But something eases. "I believe in things you can feel but not see." He nudges the fallen leaf back to me, his knuckles grazing the counter. "And in doing work right."

"Two noble creeds," I say. My voice is lighter than the weight settling low in my stomach. Not dread—a spark, sudden and secret.

A customer barges in with the force of a weather front, bringing cold air and louder conversation. Ethan steps aside, makes room without making fuss, and gives me the smallest nod as he disappears through a door that sticks slightly on the frame. He'll fix that, I think without knowing how I know.

Morag leans conspiratorial over the counter. "He's as gruff as a thistle and twice as dependable. Built these shelves. Helps half the town without keepin' tally. If your cottage door sulks in the rain, he'll sort it."

"I don't know what needs fixing yet," I say, still feeling the wake of him.

"You'll know. Glenkeld tells ye." She taps the book in my hand—Highland Lore and Harvest Tales—and rings me up. "And it listens back, if you listen first."

I step into the afternoon with the book under my arm and a candle that smells like blackberry and peat in my bag. The sun has slid lower, pouring through the gap between hills in a benediction. The square has shifted, too, changing costumes. The stalls are half-built for the weekend market, lanterns half-strung, as if the town is winking mid-prank. A child chases a paper leaf like it's a gold coin. The bakery sells out of doughnuts with the ferocious cheer of a successful heist.

I walk the path that skirts the burn and find the right rock to sit on. Water slips past like whispered plans. Up the slope, gorse pricks the sky. Somewhere to the east, the sea is doing its endless work on its endless edge. I breathe until my shoulders loosen. A soft hum threads through the air, under the known noises of town—like the sound a cat makes sunning itself—not literal—close enough, to make my skin aware of it, to nudge my pulse into a curious sync with the world around me.

When the light leans toward gold, I turn for Muir Farm. The lane out of town smells like damp earth and last-cut hay. A sign hand-lettered in green paint points the way: Pick Yer Own — Pay Honest — Mind the Geese. Beyond a low stone wall, pumpkins spill in rows across a field, their vines grey-green and papery, leaves like crumpled hands. Children dart between them, wielding little saws with the solemnity of surgeons. A woman with a camera kneels to photograph a toddler half-buried in gourds.

The geese are stationed by the gate like feathery border patrol. Their eyes are small and calculating. I buy a bag of feed from the honesty box and present tribute. "I come in peace," I murmur, scattering pellets like an acolyte. The lead goose hisses and then, magnanimously, allows me entry.

Pumpkins announce themselves as personalities. Some are squat and defiant, some tall and awkward, some freckled like they've been kissed repeatedly by careless stars. I trail my fingers across cool ridges, letting the field choose me. At the far end where the hedge leans in, I find mine: medium-large, deep orange, stem in the shape of a question mark. When I set my palm on it, a fizz of rightness leaps into my hand and settles low and warm, like the first sip of good whisky.

"You," I tell it, aware of being ridiculous and not caring. "You're coming home."

"Bit early to be talkin' to them," says a voice behind me, dry and low, "though I suppose it doesnae hurt."

Something inside me understands the voice before I turn. I knew he'd be here—don't ask how. The world has a way of bringing certain people back around until you admit you're paying attention.

Ethan stands a few feet away, rope slung over one shoulder, flannel open over a faded T-shirt. The sleeves are shoved to his forearms, revealing the kind of wrists carpenters have in poems. His hair looks like wind ran a hand through it. The geese, traitors, are pretending they like him.

"Only the special ones," I say, straightening. The field smells of damp earth and the soft iron tang of approaching evening. "I don't play favourites, but if I did…"

His mouth makes that almost-smile again, as if generosity is a language he understands but doesn't speak casually. "New folk always pick the pretty ones," he says, crouching to test the stem on an off-kilter pumpkin nearby. His hands move with a certainty that makes my throat tight. He flips open a penknife, cuts the stem in one clean, considerate motion, and sets the pumpkin upright like he's helped it find itself.

"And locals pick…" I prompt.

"Character." He lifts his eyes to mine. "Holds a candle better."

I look down at my pumpkin, which is outrageously symmetrical and therefore suspect. "I'll teach mine resilience," I promise. "Life will scuff it soon enough."

"Aye." He considers me—really looks, as if measuring dimensions I can't see. "You settling in at No. 7?"

"You knew it was No. 7?"

"Morag told half the town a fortnight ago," he says, not apologetic. "You'll find secrets go further on the wind here."

I huff a laugh. "Good thing I've got nothing to hide." My smile tilts. "Aside from the toad thing."

His brows lift a fraction. "Pardon?"

"An ex. Metaphorical amphibian. I left him to his pond."

He studies me a heartbeat longer, then nods like I've passed a test I didn't know I was taking. "If ye want that one delivered," he says, chin tipping toward my chosen pumpkin, "I'll be goin' past Rowan Lane after I've seen to Mrs. Baxter's fence. Flatbed's half full."

I should accept. Sensible women accept help from men with trucks and agreeable forearms. But some stubborn kernel inside me wants to prove I can carry the things I choose. "I can manage," I say lightly. "Unless the geese have a union and an ankle-quota."

"They keep a ledger," he deadpans. "You paid tribute. They'll let ye pass." His gaze drops to my hands. "Mind your lift."

"Engineer," I say. "I know leverage." It comes out more flirt than fact. Heat edges my cheeks. I crouch, slide my hands under the pumpkin, brace. It's heavier than expected, a pleased sort of weight, as if it enjoys being wanted.

The pumpkin wobbles. Ethan steps in without crowding, steadying it with a palm. His skin grazes mine—hot, work-rough, a spark like a struck match jumping straight to somewhere tender. For a second the entire world narrows to that contact: the warm press of his hand, the low hum of the field, the ridiculous thud of my heart drumming oh. His eyes flick to mine, and there's a softening—subtle, but there—like the first crack in ice on a thawing loch.

"I've got it," I say, steadier than I feel.

He releases at once, as if he knows about pride as well as pumpkins. "Aye."

I heft the thing against my hip and start down the row, vines brushing my boots. The field is a chorus of small noises—children negotiating the ethics of wheelbarrows, adults arguing gently about soup recipes, geese muttering like disapproving aunts. At the gate, I add a little extra to the honesty box because kindness is a currency I want to spend here.

When I turn back, Ethan is already moving down another row, knife glinting, rope coiled like a patient snake. He doesn't look my way. I don't wave. The not-looking feels like its own kind of attention, like leaving doors open without announcing it.

The walk back to Rowan Lane is a sagging triumph. My arms tremble by the last turn, and I laugh breathlessly at myself because it feels good to ache from something simple. I set the pumpkin on my step with exaggerated ceremony. The fox knocker approves, doing that impossible wink again—not literal—close enough. "He helped," I tell it.

Inside, I light the blackberry-and-peat candle and put the kettle on. The cottage gathers around me like a shawl. I open my laptop and actually answer two emails, because real life still exists and I prefer my bank account not to panic. But when I look up and out, the lane has shifted into its evening dress—lanterns lit, shadows deepening, voices soft and close. The window reflects a version of me I like better than the one I left: sweater sleeves shoved up, hair loosened by the weather, smile honest.

On impulse, I push the window open. Cold slides in, crisp and bright. Somewhere up the street, someone laughs low and easy. A dog's tags jingle. The candle flame flutters and then steadies—a soft whoomph that feels like a yes—as if taking a breath—not literal—close enough.

"Hello," I say to the night, to myself, to whatever hums here under the ordinary. "I'm Samantha. I want something true."

Footsteps scuff the cobbles outside. A tall shape passes the hedge—broad shoulders, familiar gait, the tilt of a head that looks toward my open window without stopping. Ethan's shadow crosses my pumpkin. The candle flares again, only a fraction, like applause a theatre gives itself when the curtain falls right.

I don't call to him. He doesn't knock. But a line has been drawn—chalk on stone, bright and thin and certain. Tomorrow there will be the café to discover properly, and the market stalls to wriggle through, and Morag's gossip to pretend I don't want. Tomorrow I might "accidentally" take the long way past the wood-shop. Tomorrow, I might ask him what he believes in when he's not guarding the answer.

For tonight, I curl on the sofa with my folklore book and a bowl of soup I didn't know I could make out of onions, a potato, and stubbornness. The chapter is about bargains made at the turn of seasons, about doors that learn your hands, about geese who keep watch because somebody ought to. It's about how magic—if it exists—doesn't rush. It looks like care. It sounds like a careful voice saying aye when you say I've got it. It feels like a warm palm steadying yours, then letting go.

—not literal—close enough.

Chapter 2 — Sawdust & Sunlight

Ethan's POV

The bell over Morag's door has a particular ring when it's cold out—metal sharper, sound carrying further down the square. I'm halfway through rehanging the warped hinge, shoulder to the frame and chisel in my hand, when it sings like that. The draft knifes through the shop and brings the outside with it: cinnamon from the bakery, wet wool, a sting of loch-cold air that wakes every inch of skin under my shirt.

"Mind the floorboards by the poetry," I say without looking up. "They bite if ye step wrong."

"I'll be careful," says a voice that's sunlight and mischief at once.

I do look up then.

She's got wind-painted cheeks and hair the colour of good honey, loosened by the day. Samantha. The lass from No. 7. The one who asked me if I believed in magic as if it were a reasonable opening gambit in a bookshop. The one who carried a pumpkin bigger than her common sense because pride makes mules of us all.

She stands where the light from the front window spills warm across the rugs, fingers drifting over spines like she's greeting old friends. Dust motes dance in the beam around her, and for a moment the shop goes quiet in a way I feel rather than hear, like the whole room is holding its breath to see if I'm daft enough to say the wrong thing.

Morag is, of course, delighted. "Samantha, hen! I've just had in the new MacLeod—witches and weather and men who deserve neither." She winks at me as if I'm the latter, which is unfair to men and weather both. "Ethan, if ye ruin my door I'll hang you in its place."

"It's the frame that's wrong, not the door," I tell her, because truth matters even in trivial things. I set the chisel, persuade the swollen jamb to behave, and test the swing. The door opens and closes like it's meant to. Do the job right and you don't have to do it twice. Da's voice, twenty years gone, rides up out of the muscle memory as it always does when wood yields honest.

Samantha takes a step and avoids the treacherous board without being told which one it is. Not luck. She pays attention. I tuck that away with the other things I'm not supposed to notice: the way she wraps her scarf as if she likes being held; the tiny chip on the rim of the mug she carried last night when I passed No. 7 and didn't stop; the fact that she talks to pumpkins and houses as if listening were as important as saying.

She finds the folklore shelf—of course—and takes down a new hardback with a fox on the dust jacket. When she turns, she catches me looking. I should pretend I was watching the hinge settle. I don't. I'm not a liar, even to myself.

"Did you win your battle with the geese?" I ask, because I am, despite evidence to the contrary, capable of conversation.

"I negotiated a treaty." She moves toward the counter, smile tucked into the corner of her mouth like a secret. "Full diplomatic immunity granted to pumpkin-bearers. I won't push my luck."

"Wise." I wipe a smear of sawdust from my palm onto my jeans. It leaves a pale print that looks like a ghost hand claiming me. "You carried that great lump home yourself?"

"Engineer," she says, mock-solemn. "I know leverage."

It lands like a touch. Not the wrong sort. Just the sort that makes a man aware of his edges—the places where you end if you're unlucky, and begin if you're brave.

"Ethan," Morag snaps her fingers. "Tell her about the lantern walk Saturday."

"It's just the market getting above itself," I say, but I oblige. "They turn off the streetlamps for an hour after dusk. Everyone brings their own light—paper lanterns, jars with candles, headlamps if you're a coward."

Samantha's eyes lift in that keen way again, as if she's tracking the thought all the way to where it ends. "That sounds like my favourite kind of ridiculous. Are there rules?"

"Don't set the thatch alight. Don't trip over your neighbour." I pretend to think. "Don't look at the moon too long or you'll see what it's thinking and regret it."

She laughs, quick and real, and Morag beams like she did that on purpose. Maybe she did. People like Morag arrange the world so we fall into the right pockets without knowing it's been arranged.

"I'll bring a lantern," Samantha says. "Or a jar. Or a laptop with a flashlight app if I'm feeling brave."

"Bring something with a handle," I hear myself say. "Your hands'll be busy with a paper bag from the bakery."

There's a beat where we both stand there like we're listening to the same far-off instrument. Then she tips her chin, and the sunlight does a trick on her cheekbone that digs its finger right under the rib I keep for grudges and carefulness.

"Noted," she says softly.

I should go. I have Mrs. Baxter's fence to see to before rain decides to make a liar of the forecast. The posts have rotted at the base, and if I don't brace them today, she'll call me at midnight when the sheep decide her vegetable patch looks like a nightclub.

But I linger long enough to watch Morag wrap Samantha's book, fussy as a mother cat. Samantha tucks the parcel under her arm like treasure. When she walks out, the bell rings, and a curl of cold sneaks under my collar. The door closes on the faintest whiff of her shampoo—something like rosemary and a better season.

"Don't," Morag says, not unkind, as she watches me watch the shut door.

"Don't what?"

"Don't tell yourself the old story." She leans her elbows on the counter. "Ye're not your father's temper or your brother's bad choices. You're a man with hands that mend. Let them."

21

I bristle out of habit. "I've work."

"Then do it," she says, satisfied that she's planted the burr and it will ride along until it finds skin. "And mind your heart while you're at it."

I take my tools and step into a square that looks like a pocket-watch someone keeps polishing out of pride. The sky is rinsed blue and thin with cold; clouds snag on Ben Carna like wool on wire. The bakery's window fogs and clears, fogs and clears, people inside moving like lanterns behind rice paper. Children practice with tiny brooms for the festival parade, whacking everything within reach into good behaviour. Somewhere a hammer keeps time. It's mine, I realise, belatedly, because I've already started walking toward Mrs. Baxter's.

Work is the easiest place to be when thinking gets loud. Wood speaks if you listen: where it wants to split, where it'll carry weight, where rot has eaten the courage out of it and you've to cut back to what's honest. I sink new concrete around the worst of the posts, set braces, shave a stubborn gate rail until it swings easy. Mrs. Baxter brings tea that's half sugar and all affection. She asks nothing, which is her best kindness.

By the time I'm done, the light's slanting toward evening. Smoke threads up from a dozen chimneys, and the square puts on its lanterns the way a man rolls his sleeves: not showy, just getting ready for the business of the night. I tell myself to go home to the quiet of the woodshop behind my place where slabs of ash and oak wait like dogs who trust I'll take them out.

Instead, I end up turning the long way by Rowan Lane.

I don't plan to glance at No. 7. I do. The blue door is a new sky in the dim, the brass fox knocker smug. The pumpkin on the step is the exact shade of a good decision. The front window is cracked an inch; yellow light spills out and catches the white of a page turning. I keep walking. Of course I do. I'm good at that part—motion in place of choice.

At the corner, my phone rasps in my pocket. Hamish: ye alive or has a goose killed ye? I snort and thumb back Alive. Geese sworn in as peacekeepers. He fires back three knife emojis and a heart. Brothers. They're a curse and a blessing you can't put down.

Fine. Home. The woodshop breathes easier than houses do—sap-dry air, resin and steel, saw-teeth gleaming in their rack. I run my palm over the bench and feel the day's temper settle into something useful. I plane an ash board for a shelf order, curl after pale curl lifting like the shavings are telling me a soft joke only woodworkers get. I cut true, sand until the grain rises, oil it until the figure comes up like a ghost in a photograph. It's good work. It's a way to make a body quiet and a mind honest.

But quiet isn't the same as alone, and honest isn't the same as untouched.

The image keeps offering itself whether I invite it or not: her in Morag's front window, hair lit up like the late sun caught it and forgot to let go. Her mouth shaping engineer like a spell, amused with herself and braver than is sensible.

The way she lifted that pumpkin like she meant it, and the jolt I got when my hand covered hers to steady the weight. A daft thing to fixate on, a moment as small as a hinge shifting true. But houses hang on hinges. So do some lives.

I shut up the shop and, because I'm ridiculous, walk back toward the square with no good reason I'm willing to confess to.

Glenkeld has edged into its evening self: windows gone golden, the pub's sign creaking, a tune from a fiddle pushing around the corners with the smell of stew. I step into Morag's again on the excuse of returning the spare hinge screws I don't need. She accepts them like I've brought her a firstborn.

"She went to the hill," Morag says, as if my errand were ever about screws. "The path behind the burn. There's a view that makes a soul decide whether it wants to stay."

"It's her choice," I say, hearing the gravel in my own voice.

"Aye," Morag answers sweetly. "And still."

I find myself on the path because it's where my feet go when my head's a mess. The burn is a transparent ribbon between its stones; the heather on the hillside wears the first frost at its tips like a necklace. The climb is nothing, really, but my lungs open as if I've done something earned. At the bend where the wind comes straight off the water, I see her.

She's perched on a rock with her knees tucked up, a paper-wrapped book beside her, the town spread below like a map a child coloured without keeping inside the lines.

Autumn in Glenkeld: Pumpkins & Firelight

Lanterns are already beginning in the square—pinpricks at first, then more, then more—until it looks like someone scattered embers and the cobbles decided to hold them—not literal—close enough.

I should clear my throat. I should scuff a boot. Instead, I stand a breath back, not hiding but not announcing, and watch her look at the place I have loved since I was too small to know what love was. She doesn't fidget. She doesn't fill the air with talk to make herself brave. She does what the good ones do: she listens.

The wind pushes a curl across her cheek. Without thinking, I step the last two paces and hold out my handkerchief. Old-fashioned, aye. Useful, also aye.

She startles, then smiles when she sees it's me. "Is this where you bring all the new people? Show them the view and warn them about the geese?"

"Only the ones who look like they'll listen," I say, because the truth is easier than cleverness tonight.

She takes the handkerchief, presses it to the tip of her nose. There's a ridiculous spike of tenderness in my chest at the sight—like the urge a man has to set a wobbly table steady just because he can. "I keep finding you," she says. "Or do you keep finding me?"

"Glenkeld's not big." I hook a thumb at the town. "And it folds in on itself at the edges until all the paths touch."

"That sounds like magic," she says, soft.

I sit on the rock a polite distance away, our shoulders not quite aligning. The wind worries at my jacket and brings her scent to me—rosemary and—as daft as it sounds—warm paper. "You asked me if I believed in it."

"I did." She slants me a look. "Did you answer?"

"I said I believe in things you can feel and not see." I look down at my hands. They're clean, but the lines of a day's work stay drawn in the skin no matter how you scrub. "And in doing work right. Both seem to be the only kinds that last."

She nods like that sits well in her. "Doing things right. That's a nice creed. Mine is 'don't break what you can mend, mend what you broke, and carry the heavier side of the box.'" Her mouth quirks. "Sometimes literally."

"You carried the heavier side this morning." The words are out before I decide if I'm allowed them. "At the bookshop. You took the silence."

She looks at me, straight and unflinching. "You looked like you needed someone to carry it for a minute."

There it is again—the hinge shifting. The way a door that's been hard to open suddenly swings easy and you realise you've been leaning wrong all along.

Below us, a pocket of lanterns swells and drifts as a group head from the bakery toward the square, laughter trailing behind like ribbon. The moon, not yet full, pulls itself up from behind the hill and sets the frost on the heather to low fire.

"You staying?" I ask, trying to sound like it doesn't matter.

"As long as it takes," she says, and I know I've heard that from her before, and I know I'll hear it again until we both agree what it is. She tips her head, considering me. "Are you going to keep warning me about geese?"

"Every day until you forget," I say. "Then I'll remind you."

She smiles. It's not the bright one she gives strangers. It's smaller and more dangerous and makes a hot, clean want run through me I have no business indulging. Wanting isn't the sin. The trouble is in what you do with it after. I have learned that the hard way and more than once.

"I should get back," she says after a time, not moving. "I told my laptop I'd introduce it to your Scottish Wi-Fi."

"Bring your jar on Saturday," I say, standing. "I'll make sure you don't set yourself on fire."

"That's very chivalrous."

"It's very practical." I hold a hand out without thinking and she takes it without hesitation. "Say when," I murmur. "Now," she says, bracing. Her fingers are warm; mine know exactly how to close around them. I pull her up, and because balance is a fickle friend, she steps closer for a beat longer than necessary. Wind. Frost. Lanterns. The soft scrape of her boot shifting on stone. The part of me that wants reaches for what I'm not ready to take, and the part of me that's careful keeps us both whole.

"See you, Ethan," she says, letting go.

"Aye," I answer, because that word does a lot of work if you let it.

We walk down the path together without brushing once, which feels like both a triumph and a loss, and when we part at the footbridge, she looks over her shoulder and catches me looking again. I don't look away. If a thing is true, you may as well let it be seen.

Back in my shop, I light the stove and set the kettle on its iron ring. The little space fills with the good smells—tea and oil and the faint ghost of shavings burned last winter when the wind found a seam. I sit on the bench with my hands open on my knees and feel the edges of the day settle into place.

There's work tomorrow. There's always work—hinges and shelves and fences and small honest things that keep bigger things standing. But tonight, there's also the knowledge of a woman who listens, who carries, who asked me about magic and then didn't laugh when I told her the only true answer I own.

I put a mark in my ledger for Mrs. Baxter's fence, and another, smaller, in the part of my head where I measure fewer tangible jobs. Lantern walk Saturday, I write there in a voice that sounds uncomfortably like Morag's. Jar with handle. Keep her hands free.

It's a daft thing, maybe, to plan for hands that aren't mine. It's a dangerous thing to notice how perfectly one might fit another. But there are dafter, more dangerous things than making sure there's room for light.

I reach the stove, finish the tea, and let the quiet come on. The town hums through the walls the way a well-built house does when you've set it true. Outside, somewhere, a fox barks once, neat as a nail tapped home. I think of the blue door and the winking knocker and a pumpkin that will hold a candle steady when the wind asks it hard questions.

"Aye," I tell the empty room, and feel the word land where it needs to.

Chapter 3 — The Pumpkin Patch
Samantha's POV

The whole town smells like cinnamon and cider.

I follow the trail of it down the lane, drawn as if my body has decided it doesn't matter what my brain thinks, I'm going where the sugar is. The air is crisp, the kind that nips at the tip of your nose but makes your lungs greedy for more. Gold and amber leaves cling stubbornly to branches overhead, swirling down in lazy spirals when the wind plucks too hard. The cobblestones crunch with grit from fallen acorns. I'm half-convinced Glenkeld exists in permanent October, like the whole place signed a pact with autumn and never looked back.

The pumpkin patch spreads across the edge of town in an explosion of orange. The field rolls wide, dotted with pumpkins of every possible size: squat ones like fat coins, elegant ones stretched tall and stately, lopsided characters that look like they're in the middle of telling jokes. A wooden cart near the gate sells cider in steaming cups and paper bags of cinnamon-sugar doughnuts. Lanterns strung on crooked poles line the path, already lit though the sun's still up; their wicks give a soft whoomph as the breeze nudges them, glow warm against the blue-grey sky—not literal—close enough.

Children dart between rows, shrieking with delight when they find "the one." Parents trail behind, pretending to complain but smiling like fools. Somewhere near the back, a man in a kilt strums a guitar, the soft notes threading through the laughter. My heart does a little skip at the sound, and for the first time in a long time, I don't feel like an outsider. I feel like I've stepped into something waiting for me.

I buy a cider, the paper cup hot against my palms. The first sip tastes like everything good about autumn—apples, spice, firelight, comfort—and I sigh so hard the vendor laughs. "First time at Muir's?" she asks, tucking change into her apron.

"First time anywhere like this," I admit. "Back home it was supermarkets and plastic bins of pumpkins."

"Not here," she says proudly. "Every one grown in this soil. Pick yer own. Just mind the geese."

There it is again. I glance toward the far fence where a gaggle of white geese patrol like surly guards, necks stretched, eyes mean. They honk at a boy who gets too close and he yelps, running back to his mother. I salute them with my cider and decide tribute is absolutely the way forward.

I wander between rows, cradling my cup, letting the crisp air and the murmur of voices weave around me. Pumpkins crowd my feet, their skins cool and smooth when I nudge them with my boot. I crouch to study a particularly round one, stem curled like a corkscrew. Too perfect. I want something with a little more story.

That's when I hear it: the scrape of boots on soil, the steady rhythm of someone who belongs here. My skin prickles before I even look up.

Ethan.

Of course. Tall, broad-shouldered, rope looped over one arm, a penknife glinting in his hand. He's dressed for the chill—flannel open over a dark tee, sleeves pushed up to reveal the strength in his forearms. His hair is a little windswept, as though the breeze itself wanted to muss him. And those storm-grey eyes… well. They find me before I can look away, steady and unflinching, like he knew I'd be here all along.

For a ridiculous heartbeat, I think I've conjured him. The thought is too dangerous, so I cover it with bravado. "You again. Do you haunt all the pumpkin patches, or just this one?"

"Just this one." His mouth curves in that almost-smile of his, the one that feels like a secret only I get to see. "And you."

I take another sip of cider to cover the way my pulse skips. The heat has nothing to do with the drink. "I've been warned about the geese. Twice now."

"Aye." He glances toward the fence where the feathered army still patrols. "They're merciless. But they respect tribute."

"I'll remember that." I crouch again, brushing my fingers over a medium-sized pumpkin with a stem like a question mark. "What about this one? Good character, or just pretty?"

He steps closer—too close—and crouches beside me. His hand joins mine on the pumpkin, rough skin against my softer palm; heat pools where skin meets skin. The contact jolts through me like a current. My breath catches. He doesn't move right away, and for a long moment we're both touching it, our hands brushing in the cool dusk. The world tilts: the children's laughter, the strum of guitar, the geese honking—all of it fades until there's only this heat, this awareness, this man.

"Solid," he says finally, voice low. His thumb strokes once along the stem before he pulls back. "Would carve clean. Hold a candle steady."

Something in my chest answers to that—like he's not just talking about pumpkins. I swallow hard. "Then it's mine."

"You'll carry it yourself?" His tone is teasing but edged with challenge.

"I've done it before." I lift my chin, remembering the ache in my arms from yesterday. "I'm stronger than I look."

Grey eyes catch mine, unreadable but intent. "Aye," he says softly. "I reckon you are."

The words land heavy in my chest, warming places I didn't know were cold.

We walk together through the rows, the air between us charged. Our hands brush once, twice—accidents that feel anything but. Each time, my stomach flips. He doesn't move away, doesn't apologise. Just lets it happen, as if the space between us belongs to both of us now.

By the cart, I set the pumpkin on the scale and pay honestly. Ethan lingers a step behind, watching, as though he's making sure I don't drop it— or maybe as though he wants to see if I'll ask for help. I don't. Pride and nerves are powerful motivators.

When the vendor hands me the pumpkin, I cradle it awkwardly against my hip. It's heavier than I expected, and I wobble. Ethan's hand is instantly there, steadying the weight, his palm warm against mine. "Say when," he breathes. "Now," I manage. That spark again, sharp and undeniable. My breath snags as I look up at him, and for one dangerous second it feels like the world holds its breath with me.

"You've got it," he murmurs.

"I've got it," I echo, though my voice is thinner than I want.

He lets go slowly, reluctantly. The loss is immediate. I carry the pumpkin to the path, my arms burning, my chest buzzing. At the gate, the geese eye me but let me pass. I toss them a grateful nod. Ethan follows, silent but close, his presence a steady shadow at my side.

At the edge of the field, I pause to adjust the pumpkin against my hip; my pulse drums under his steadier calm. My fingers ache, but I don't admit it. Instead, I glance up at him, trying for casual. "Do you always appear where I am, or am I just lucky?"

"Glenkeld's not that big." His eyes linger on me a second too long, and the corner of his mouth twitches. "But aye. Lucky."

The air between us crackles like kindling. My heart hammers so hard I'm sure he hears it. For one dizzy instant, I think he might close the distance, might lean down, might—

A child shrieks somewhere behind us, chasing a runaway pumpkin. The moment shatters. I grip my pumpkin tighter, laugh too quickly, and head back toward the square. Ethan falls into step beside me, silent, steady, as if nothing happened. As if everything did.

Somewhere up on the brae, a fox barks once, neat as a nail tapped home.

Chapter 4 — Golden Light, Sharp Edges
Ethan's POV

By the time the sun lets go of the hills, Glenkeld has turned itself inside out for the weekend market—stalls open like bright mouths, lanterns strung from lintel to lintel, the square powdered with flour and laughter. Someone's hung a chain of tiny glass bottles along Morag's awning, each with a candle stub burning down; they make a sound like a soft chime when the breeze tests them, as if light itself could ring—not literal—close enough.

I'm meant to be done for the day. The shop's stove is banked, the plane iron set, the ledger closed with the neatness of a man who likes to leave the edges true. But the square is a magnet and I'm iron tonight. Or maybe I'm just a fool who wants to stand where he might see her without admitting that's the reason.

I skirt the bakery queue, pretend to study a new set of iron hooks at the smith's stall, nod to Hamish where he's failing to flirt with Katie the florist. The air is cinnamon and peat and the briny thread of the loch. Children streak past with lanterns made from turnips and jars. Music strikes up—a fiddle and a bodhrán—and people begin to sway without deciding to.

And there she is.

Samantha stands near the cider cart with a paper cup in both hands, the steam ribboning up around her face like the place has decided to draw attention to her on purpose. The lanterns throw warm coins across her hair; her scarf is the colour of rowan berries and makes the line of her throat look like something a painter might boast about when he's drunk. She's listening to an old man explain the proper way to mull cider, head tipped, mouth soft with amusement.

I'm looking before I can stop myself. She feels it—some people do—and turns. The first second is the worst: recognition, the small lift of her mouth, the thing in my chest that kicks against the ribs like it wants out. I start to lift a hand, think better of it, and move toward her like I was coming anyway.

"Did you bring your jar?" I ask. It's ridiculous, how steady I sound.

She lifts her cup in answer, eyes bright. "I upgraded. I was promised cinnamon sticks and thinly veiled community gossip."

"You'll get both and more trouble besides." I take the stall's second cup when the vendor thrusts it at me, money already down because Morag has told everyone to feed me when I forget. The first sip burns the bad out of a day I didn't know had any left. "Careful of the gossip. It sticks."

"Maybe I want it to." She blows across her cider. The steam kisses her cheek. I have to look away.

The lights over the stall gutter and then give a soft whoomph, like a heartbeat—not literal—close enough. I don't believe in omens, only in care and craft and the way a house sounds when it's set true. Still—there's a charge to the air, a hum in the wire of the evening that feels like the pause before rain.

We drift along the stalls because it's easier to move than to stand still and be obvious. She picks up a skein of wool and rubs it against her wrist, smiling at the softness. I test the balance on a new chisel the smith's brought in, decide it's worth what he's asking, and buy it before I can find an excuse not to. At the apiarist's table, she lets a drop of heather honey melt on her tongue. The little noise she makes does something to my head that's not my finest hour. I cough and pretend interest in a beeswax polish I don't need.

"Do you always look like you're guarding something?" she asks, light and not.

"Do I?" I feign innocence. Guarding is easier than giving. It's also lonelier.

"You watch a room," she says softly. "Like a carpenter checks a frame for load bearing. Not a bad thing. Just true."

Fair's fair. "And you come at the world at a run, then remember to breathe halfway through."

She laughs, quick and clean. "Also, true."

We end up at the square's edge under a run of golden bulbs strung low enough to warm the hair on the tops of our heads. The band shifts to a tune meant for feet. Couples sway. Children whirl themselves into dizzy puddles. Someone passes with a tray of oatcakes and cheese and we each take one because it's what you do when abundance is making a show of itself and there's no sense in being rude.

"Sit?" I suggest, nodding to the low wall by the kirk, its stone warmed by the day and holding onto the memory. We take the middle of it like we agreed ahead of time, shoulders close enough that a misjudged breath will put us touching. "Say when," I murmur before I can think. "Near," she says, steady as a promise. I set my cup on the wall to cool. She keeps hers in both hands as if it's safer that way.

"So," she says, like a woman who's decided to step over a line, "tell me your worst thing and your best thing."

"That's a wide road."

"It narrows. Worst first. I'll go too." She's looking at me in that way that doesn't flinch. "I like skipping small talk. It wastes time we could be using on good talk."

The past rises because she asked it to. I take a breath and choose the words I can live with. "Worst thing is when temper runs in a family and you keep it on a leash so long your hands bleed, and still, it sometimes gets its teeth into what you love." My voice stays even. It always does. "Best thing is wood that tells you what it wants to be and your hands knowing how to listen."

She doesn't look away, doesn't make a sympathetic noise that would cost me twice. She just nods like a craftsman offered truth as a fair trade. "Worst thing," she says after a beat, "is mistaking a person's charm for their character and then apologising for your own boundaries until you can't hear yourself anymore." Her mouth quirks with something that isn't quite humour. "Best thing is building something—

I mean code, but also anything—that works because you were patient and stubborn at the same time."

"Both take hands," I say. "Even when it looks like a head's job."

Her shoulder bumps mine. Accidental. Not accidental. The lights overhead flare and settle again, and I am not a man to read meaning into electricity, but my blood hears the music change key.

"Why Glenkeld?" I ask, because if I keep thinking about the distance between her mouth and mine, I'll forget how to speak. "You could work anywhere."

"Because this place feels like it's listening." She looks out at the square—the lanterns, the laughter, Morag talking with her whole body, Hamish dancing with Katie and pretending his boots aren't too big for it. "Because it's October here even when it's not. Because I wanted to believe in…in care, I guess. In people who fix things, quietly."

That last lands so cleanly I almost look away. "We've our share of noise," I say, because humility is a habit. "But aye. There's care."

We sit in the warmth and the dark awhile, letting the sound of a town at its best settle into our bones. She tells me about a project she's building—payment logic that keeps failing at the edge cases because edge cases are all any system ever is. I tell her about the shelf order I'm finishing, a reading nook for a boy who needs a place where noise is a choice. We don't brag. We talk like people who know work is its own language and not one everyone speaks.

Then she turns and the movement brings her closer than it should. There's not one thing that makes it happen—nobody bumps us, the music doesn't swell, the wind doesn't shove. We simply end up too near under a string of small suns, cider and honey on our breath, the little space between us full of the worst best idea I've had in a long time.

Her eyes tip to my mouth. Mine do a poor job of pretending not to. It would be the easiest thing in the world to end the distance—a small lean, a smaller closing of the thinking parts. The lantern light paints the bow of her lip in gold. Her chest rises once, careful. The first notes of a silence fall around us like snow.

I could. I want. I don't.

A moment is a hinge. This one swings both ways: toward wanting and toward what happens after. I know the weight of afterward. Desire isn't the problem. It's the edges—sharp, hungry—that turn to harm when you pretend you don't have them.

I draw breath—slow, a sober man putting the cork back in the bottle—and turn my head the smallest degree so that the kiss lands where it can't: on the near edge of her cheek, soft and brief, a touch any neighbour might claim was friendly if they were blind and foolish.

She stills. Not hurt. Not slighted. Surprised. Then something flickers through her—disappointment, yes, but not the kind that sours. More like the ache in a muscle that wants the heavier weight and knows it'll come when it should.

"Right," she says, barely above the music. "You're careful."

"Too much sometimes," I admit, because I won't insult either of us with less.

"Okay." She nods once, eyes lowering for a heartbeat. When she looks up, there's a new understanding in them, the kind you only get from being told not now by someone who means not yet. "Okay."

I make myself breathe like a man who isn't standing in a fire he lit on purpose. I tip my cup to my lips and drink the last sweet mouthful, buying a second to get my voice right. "Come Saturday," I say, and my words are steady. "Lantern walk. The town turns off the lights at dusk and we try not to trip over our own feet."

"Will you be there?" she asks, like she doesn't already know.

"Aye." My mouth does the thing it resists and tips into a real smile. "I'll make sure you don't set yourself alight."

"That's very practical of you."

"It's self-interest. You'd take the whole square with you."

She laughs, head tipping back. The sound goes into me and finds every place I've kept empty for safety and sets a chair there. She reaches up then—slow, so I could stop it if I meant to—and brushes her thumb along my cheek where the almost-kiss almost was; my pulse kicks under her thumb. Not claiming. Not scolding. Just…thank you and damn you both.

"Not yet," she says, and the words feel like a promise more than a reprimand.

"Not yet," I agree, and the agreement tastes like the edge of something worth the waiting.

We slide off the wall and join the slow river of people. Morag catches my eye over someone's shoulder and gives me a look that says good lad and about time and don't be an idiot in three dialects. I roll my eyes at her and Samantha hides a smile behind her cup.

We walk the square twice and end up back where we began without meaning to, like the town folded its map to show us what it keeps folding toward. When we part at the top of Rowan Lane, she touches my wrist once—light, quick—and the place under her fingers burns long after she's gone.

At the shop, I set the new chisel on the bench and run a thumb along its edge. Sharp, honest, needing care. A tool that could do harm if you pretended it wouldn't. A thing you keep sheathed until the moment you mean to use it well.

I bank the stove lower and stand in the door awhile, letting the square finish its song around me. The lanterns in their glass bottles give one last soft whoomph and settle—not literal—close enough. Somewhere a fox barks once, neat as a nail tapped home. I think of a blue door and a fox knocker that winks more than brass should, of a pumpkin that will hold a candle steady, of a woman with a mouth I didn't kiss. Yet.

Careful, I tell myself. Not coward. There's a difference.

Saturday's coming. And the dark is kinder when you carry your own light.

Chapter 5 — Lanterns & Small Confessions
Samantha's POV

By late afternoon, the town hums like a kettle just before the whistle. Stalls bloom along the square like bright mushrooms after rain: jars of jam glowing like stained glass, skeins of wool coiled in sherbet colours, knives that catch the sun and wink, stacks of oatcakes banded with twine. Paper moons sway overhead. Children stamp around with home-carved turnip lanterns with gnarled little faces and snaggle-teeth, while the grown-ups pretend, they aren't thrilled to bits.

Morag presses a bundle into my hands the moment she sees me. "Here ye are, hen—plaid ribbon for your jar and a biscuit to keep you upright." The biscuit is the size of my palm, sugared and perfumed with lemon; the ribbon is tartan red as rowan berries.

"My aesthetic has been seen," I tell her, and tie the ribbon around the wire handle of the jar I've brought. Inside, a beeswax candle waits like a small, patient heart.

"'Course it has." She leans conspiratorial over the counter. "If a tall lad with sawdust in his hair happens by, tell him I've the screws he forgot and the sense he needs."

"Noted." Warmth slips under my skin and settles there, the kind that doesn't demand anything, just glows.

The square fills a little more with every breath. I buy hot cider because that seems to be a requirement of the evening, and then I fail to resist a cinnamon doughnut. I tell myself

I'm keeping my blood sugar stable. I tell myself nothing at all when I turn and nearly collide with a man-shaped wall of flannel and gravity.

Ethan.

"Careful," he says, steadying the cup with one hand and the doughnut with the other as if he's rescuing small planets from disastrous orbit. His fingers brush mine—barely—and the place they touch sparks heat up my arm like someone lit a fuse in my veins.

"Trying to avoid second-degree cinnamon burns," I say. "Or third-degree public embarrassment."

"We'd get you to Morag's." That almost-smile, private, reluctant, and devastating. "She keeps a salve for both."

He's carrying a lantern too, of course—a squat jar with a bail handle, glass smudged by years of use. When I look closer, there's a tiny carved notch in the wooden lid: a fox's face, just two clever strokes for eyes, one for a smile.

"You made that," I say.

"Aye." The tips of his ears pinken. "Years ago. It's…a good jar."

"It's a very good jar." I tip mine toward his. "Jar friends?"

"Jar friends," he echoes, the words catching on a laugh that escapes before he can stop it. The laugh looks good on him; it loosens something behind his eyes.

We're carried with the crowd as the hour draws near. Glenkeld has been dressing for this all day: candles lined on windowsills, strings of tiny glass bottles with tea lights swaying from Morag's awning, lanterns tucked into nooks like secret coins. The bell in the kirk tower shakes itself out; a hush rolls over the square as if someone laid a hand on the town's shoulder and said, "Listen."

The streetlights snap off.

For a breath there is only darkness and the knowledge of each other's breathing. Then the first lantern blooms, then another, then another, until the square is a constellation and we are each a star inside it. My candle catches with a soft whoomph, wick taking, flame trembling, and everyone cheers like we've discovered warmth for the first time—not literal—close enough.

"Come on," Ethan says, low, like he's talking to skittish horses. "Stay close or you'll end up in Mrs. Baxter's arms, and she'll marry ye to a sheep before you can say oatcake."

I slip to his side, the crowd folding around us, lanterns bobbing like fireflies. The band—fiddle, bodhrán, someone with a whistle—strikes up a tune that sounds like marching and dancing made a pact and met in the middle. Bodies sway. Children dart. I bump Ethan's arm; he doesn't move away. Our shoulders find an easy geography. It feels both daring and ordinary, like how you might choose to breathe and then remember you were always doing it.

We drift the square, part of a river made of light. Hamish—Ethan's brother, who greets me now with cheerful conspiracy—swings past with Katie from the florist; he tips his lantern at me as if it's a hat. Mrs. Baxter plants herself along the route like a checkpoint commander and demands to see everyone's flame. "Good," she tells me, inspecting my jar. "Steady. That one," she jerks her chin at Ethan, "burns like that too when he's not pretending he doesn't."

"Mrs. Baxter," Ethan groans, turning the colour of baked brick.

"She's right," I say without thinking. Ethan shoots me a look that's half-wounded, half-pleased, as if praise sits strange on him and he isn't sure where to put it.

We pause near the apiarist's stall where a line of jar candles turns the honey to amber lightning. The light throws patterns across Ethan's cheek, catching in his beard, gilding the stubborn curve of his mouth. I want—improbably—to press my palm there to see if he's as warm as he looks. Instead, I lift my lantern, letting the glow climb my wrist, and he leans an inch closer as if he can't decide whether he's found the edge or if there even is one.

"Tell me something true," I say.

He huffs a quiet laugh. "We started with worst and best the other night. That wasn't truth enough for ye?"

"Different truth," I insist, softer. "The kind you don't put on forms."

He thinks about it, gaze on our two flames, their light overlapping in a spill of gold—twin flames making one pool of gold on the cobbles. "When I was twelve," he says at last, "I took apart Da's clock and couldn't put it back. Sat up all night with the pieces laid out by shape and shame. He never raised his voice. He just made tea and said, 'We learn by how we mend what we break, lad.'" He swallows once. "Next morning, it ticked."

I picture it—the boy bent over gears and guilt, a man's patience sitting beside him until the world clicked back together. Something soft and fierce unfurls in me. "Then you were doomed," I say. "To fix things in a town that keeps offering you new projects."

"Aye." His smile is not reluctant this time. It's small and whole and it lands on me like a hand on my shoulder. "Your turn."

"Truth." I breathe it in with the candle smoke. "I left because I was tired of apologising for taking up space. I came because this town felt like it would ask me to take more."

He turns his head to look at me then, not the lanterns or the crowd or the curve of the square: me. "You can have the whole street," he says simply. "We'll move the fences."

The music rises, breaks, mends itself. Laughter darts and disappears. A child's lantern tips and rights. Somewhere, geese complain from their field like drunk critics. It is ridiculous to tear up in a crowd because a man offered you metaphorical property rights, and yet here we are.

"Thank you," I manage.

"Don't thank me for the obvious." His voice has rough edges and kindness in it. "Show me instead."

So, I do a foolish thing. I reach sideways until my fingers find the tips of his. He doesn't start. He doesn't grab. He just lets my hand rest there like a bird testing a branch, the bones of his knuckles steady beneath my palm. Our lanterns kiss light to light between our knees.

We stand like that through two songs and a story told by old Mr. Fergus in a whisper that somehow reaches everyone. The world tightens to the circle of glow around our feet, and beyond it, the town hums and behaves and is kind to itself in a way that makes my ribcage feel properly sized.

When the streetlights come back on, the cheer is loud enough to shake the bunting. The night remembers itself: pub doors opening like warm mouths, steam from the soup tent, a skirl of wind nosing the paper moons. The procession loosens; people become people again instead of a single creature made of light.

"Walk you home?" Ethan asks. He keeps his eyes on his lantern as if the answer might live there.

I don't play coy. "Yes."

Rowan Lane is quieter than the square, a place where voices land and go still. The sky above is the deep-dark blue that only happens when the cold has opinions. Our lanterns paint stripes along the stone walls, our shadows tall and companionable. Somewhere a fox barks once, neat as a nail tapped home. The brass fox knocker on my door will be jealous.

We fall into step easy as an exhale. Our shoulders brush. Don't brush. Brush again. He breathes, "Say when."

"Near," I say; we keep the line. Each not-exactly-accident sends that small, private spark through me until I feel lit from the inside. I could say something flippant; I could make a joke to chase off the wanting before it grows teeth. I don't. We carry the wanting like we're carrying a flame: upright, careful, no apology for the heat.

"Your jar held," he says, not because he needs to but because he wants me to know he noticed.

"So did yours," I say, and it feels like a bigger thing than jars.

We stop at my step. The pumpkin sits fat and pleased by the door, and the fox knocker catches lantern light like it's been practicing for this moment all week. The cottage behind the blue door is warm, the blackberry-and-peat candle probably burned to a stub, the kettle likely eager. I could invite him in for tea; I could set the table for something else entirely. The offer rises to my mouth and sits there like a coin on my tongue.

He must see it. He must see me debate, weigh, burn, bank. His eyes soften by an inch. "Don't set the town on fire yet," he says, smiling. "We've barely hung the lanterns up."

"Yet," I echo, and the word is a ribbon brushed along a wrist.

We set our jars side by side on the step without speaking. Twin flames, two hearts, one small ceremony. The fox knocker—brazen flirt—winks—not literal—close enough. My candle flares, then steadies with a soft whoomph, as if approving the arrangement—not literal—close enough.

"Saturday was good," I say.

"It was," he agrees, and then we laugh because it is scandalously insufficient and exactly right.

He shifts—forward, back—as if caught by two currents he trusts equally. His hand lifts, hovers near my cheek, then settles on my shoulder instead. The weight is warm and careful and entirely undoing. "I like the way you listen," he says, low enough that it's something he can take back tomorrow if he wants, though I don't think he will. "To rooms. To people. To yourself."

"I like the way you mend things," I say. "Even if it's just doors and jars and townspeople being foolish."

"Especially those," he says, and his thumb finds the ridge of my collarbone where my scarf has shifted. It doesn't stroke; it simply rests, a promise made by stillness. My pulse taps against his thumb, brazen.

We stand there a breath and another, the night playing fair. If he kissed me now, I would go whole and bright and not look back. If I kissed him now, I might never get my heart out of his hands. I feel both truths and choose neither, which is not cowardice, I decide, but an odd kind of bravery: to admit you want something and still let it ripen on the vine.

"Goodnight, Samantha," he says.

"Goodnight, Ethan."

He takes up his lantern, leaves mine to keep company with the pumpkin, and steps back into the lane. He doesn't look away as he goes. Neither do I. He turns the corner, tall shadow shrinking, light cupped in his hand like a kept secret. The wind lifts, fiddles with the ribbon on my jar, and then pockets itself.

Inside, I nudge the door shut with my hip and lean back against it, heart doing its best hummingbird. The cottage smells like beeswax and soup I don't remember making, like the kind of life you can eat with a spoon. I set water to boil and lean my forehead to the cool pane of the window, watching the flame on the step ride the draft like they're enjoying a small adventure.

"Okay," I tell the room, because rooms deserve to be told things. "We did not spontaneously combust. We carried light. We said not yet."

The fox knocker—obnoxious creature—winks again, and I swear the candle on the table answers with a polite little bow.

Later, in bed, the sound of the town is a softer animal. People peel themselves apart, lights slide to dark, footsteps diminish. My body is lit from the inside and sleeping feels like abandoning a vigil, but even lanterns have to be snuffed if you want to keep the wick. I close my eyes and see not his mouth (though, yes), but his hand cupped around flame, the way he angled his lantern away from the wind, so I didn't have to.

Not yet. But soon has a shape now. It looks like a jar with a fox etched in its lid, two flames steadying each other, the promise of a kiss hung between us like a light we both know how to tend.

Chapter 6 — Heat in the Grain

Ethan's POV

Morning comes sharp and clean, and I try to sand it down with work.

Plane. Measure. Mark. Cut. The bench is a good altar for a man who prefers prayers with shavings. Ash under my palms is cool as river stone; the blade sings; curls lift pale and perfect then break, fraying at the ends like a mind that won't keep its edge. I reset the iron, take a finer pass, and still—still—my head feeds me the same unruly pictures: her mouth in lantern light, the way she said *not yet* like a hand on the back of my neck, guiding but not pushing. The ghost of sugar on her lips. The heat that climbed my wrist when she touched me as if the touch belonged to both of us.

I set the plane down before I take an unnecessary bite out of the board. Second best to prayer is motion, so I move: sweep, stack, oil, hinge a cabinet door for Mrs. MacRae's pantry and test it five times to be certain it will swing sweet in damp weather. The stove ticks, the kettle breathes, the shop smells of resin and steel and my own clean sweat. It ought to be enough.

It isn't.

Her laugh threads through the space like a tune you don't mean to hum and find yourself whistling anyway. I wipe my palms and try again with the ash shelf, but every stroke sets off a chain reaction: long grain under hand becomes the line of her throat in lantern light; the curve of the board's edge is the bow of her lip; the warm lift of shavings is the heat that crawled up my skin when she stood close, jar between us like a tamed spark.

I nick my thumb on the chisel. Not bad. Enough to insult my pride.

"Get your head right," I tell the empty room, and the room answers with the softest creak in the rafters, old wood reminding me it is both stronger and more forgiving than men who live under it.

I dress the cut, pour tea, and pretend the steam is strong enough to fog out a certain face. It isn't that I don't know what to do with wanting. Wanting's an honest tool in the kit. It's that the edges of it can turn clever hands clumsy if you lie to yourself about how sharp they are. I don't want to nick her. I don't want to nick me. And still—my feet are ridiculous traitors and make plans without asking my permission.

"I'll be at Morag's," I tell the ledger, as if the ledger cares, and the ledger pretends to be impressed by my administrative rigour.

Morag catches me with her usual scalpel smile. "I'm not saying it out loud," she says, sliding a paper bag across the counter, "but if I were, I'd say take the biscuits and your sense with you."

"My sense?" I stuff the bag into my jacket before the shop cat gets ideas. "You've been telling me for years I've too much of it."

"Not today." She flicks a glance toward the square where a hand-lettered sign promises a bonfire at the common tonight—marshmallows, reels, bring your own cup and your better self. "This evening's for warmth and decision, Ethan-grace. Don't mistake one for the other."

"Since when d'you get mystical?"

"Since the day you learned to listen to wood." She shooes me toward the door. "Go mend something before you start brooding and scare the tourists."

I mend Mrs. MacRae's pantry without breaking anything, which is not nothing, and drink more tea than a sane man should. By midafternoon, the weather does that Scottish trick where the light is all pewter, but the air is gold. I load the flatbed with tomorrow's deliveries and tell myself—firmly—that I will go straight home.

The road past Rowan Lane is the shortest. I take it without meaning to, which is a lie I can live with.

Her blue door is a patch of sky in the day's grey; the fox knocker looks smug. The pumpkin on the step has settled into itself with that fat contentment pumpkins get when they know they belong. Through the front window—curtain pulled mostly, but not entirely, across—I see her. She's on a step stool, reaching to tie a sprig of eucalyptus to the curtain rod with twine, jumper slouched off one shoulder like the knit forgot what shoulders are for. The sliver of skin there is nothing—ordinary—except my body doesn't think so. Heat wakes across my chest, low and blunt and not at all polite.

I could keep walking. I should. My hands, however, are attached to a man with poor impulse control where certain problems are concerned. I knock once, tell the knocker to stop winking at me—not literal—close enough, and step back.

She opens, breathless from the step stool, hair caught in the twine like it wanted to be tied up there and forgot how to behave. The jumper slides a fraction more. It's a very civilised jumper. I want very uncivilised things.

"Hi," she says, a little surprised, a lot pleased. Her eyes do that warm thing they do to my insides. "Do you greet all your customers with the expression of a man who's walked into a room and forgotten why he's there?"

"Only the ones who leave rope lying around on purpose," I say, because the universe has decided to test me, and I might as well show it I can read the exam. I lift the bag from Morag. "I come bearing biscuits and judgement."

"On which side?"

"Biscuits are for you. Judgement's for me." I tip my chin at the door. "You mind if I...?"

"Fix something that isn't broken because you need to do something with your hands?" She steps back, ushering me in with a sweep that lets that jumper slip another damned millimetre. "Be my guest."

It's small inside and warm in all the right ways: candle gone to a stub, kettle humming, the smell of beeswax and cinnamon and a woman making a life she hasn't had time to be cynical about. The latch does, in fact, have play. The top hinge could take a quarter-turn. I set my bag on the table, find the right screwdriver from memory, and pretend that's the reason I'm here while we both agree not to say the other reason out loud.

"Hold this?" I ask, palm flat against the door. She steps close, presses her hand over mine, and the two of us brace it together while I tighten the top hinge. "Say when," I murmur. "Now," she says, steady. It's basic work. It feels like prayer.

Her breath warms my wrist. "You always run toward the thing you want to avoid?"

"Only when avoidance looks like a step stool and twine," I mutter, and she laughs—quiet, pleased, aware of what we're doing without forcing it to have a name yet.

I test the swing; it takes a good line now. "Better," I say.

"Better," she agrees, and doesn't let her hand leave mine where it still rests on the wood. She doesn't have to. She does it because she can.

I should step back. I should set the screwdriver down. Instead, I lean a shoulder to the jamb and let the house narrow the world until there's only her and me and the wood, we're both touching. I can smell rosemary and heat and something that's just her. The fox knocker eyes us, shamelessly.

She shifts to get past me, and I don't move fast enough on purpose. The brush of her body down my front is a spark taking a mile of fuse in a heartbeat. She breathes in, not a gasp, just that small can-you-feel-that inhale a person makes when the world sharpens. I make a sound that might be her name or a warning. I don't check.

By some miracle of character, I step back before I ruin us. "Careful," I say. It's a prayer and an apology.

She looks at me like she sees exactly what I didn't do and why. "Deliberate," she says back, correcting me. "Not careful." She reaches into the bag, breaks a biscuit, and—because the day intends to test the welds on my restraint—lifts a sugared edge to my mouth. "Taste."

I could take it with my fingers like a civilised man. I don't. I lean in and catch the bite between my teeth, heat moving through me in a straight line when her hand stays where it is, close enough that my bottom lip ghosts her thumb. Sugar melts. So does something I've kept iron-clad.

Her eyes go darker. A soft noise gets out of me that I hope the house keeps to itself. I close around her wrist—gentle, asking—and turn her hand so her sugared thumb faces me. "Dangerous," I say, last warning. Then I take the smallest, slowest taste from the pad of her thumb like a vow I mean to make good on. No more than tongue and sugar and breath, but my bones ring with it.

She swallows. The sound is pure sin. "You can't do that and say not yet," she whispers, not chiding, exactly—negotiating.

"I can if I'm going to do it right when I do it," I say, because truth is a better seduction than any lie I could invent. My hand is still on her wrist; her pulse is doing the gallop we've both been pretending we can't hear. "Tell me to go."

She doesn't. She steps in instead, slow as a tide, until her body is a warm fact against mine, until I can count her breaths and the space between them. The door is at her back; my palm finds the frame by her head. I can see the near-silent plea at the corner of her mouth and the stubbornness that makes her so impossible and so easy to love all at once.

Kiss her.

Don't.

Kiss her.

Don't.

I bend—God help me, I do—and take the place that isn't her mouth: the curve where her cheek becomes jaw, the spot that flushed under lantern light last night. I set my mouth there like a blessing and a threat. She tips her head without being told, and the sound she makes goes straight through me and wrecks my plans in every direction.

"Ethan," she says, and my name in that voice is a thing I'd build a house around.

I pull back enough to see her eyes. "Bonfire's tonight," I say, rougher than I want to be. "Edge of the common. Come."

"As if I'd miss an excuse to watch you near an open flame," she says, trying for light and not quite reaching it. "I'll bring something. Marshmallows. A fire extinguisher."

"I'll bring sense," I tell her, which is a lie and we both know it.

We stand there, suspended. The candle on the table gutters and then flares with a soft whoomph, brave little witness—not literal—close enough. The fox knocker winks because of course it does. Outside, the afternoon slides toward that bright, brittle hour before dusk when everything looks like it's made of the same metal as memory.

I let her wrist go first, because if I don't, there won't be a later and I want all the laters. She moves past me, this time when I let her, fingers brushing my hip so lightly I'd swear I imagined it if my blood didn't vouch for me.

"Thank you for fixing my definitely broken latch," she says, mouth a curve I want to put my hands on.

"Anytime," I answer, which is an obscenity of an offer given the state of me.

On the step, the air is colder than it has any right to be. I take it like a punishment and a promise. "After dark," I say. "North path."

She leans the door against her shoulder, gaze on mine, soft and sure as a bruise you keep pressing to remember you're alive. "After dark."

I go before I do what I know I can do and we both decide to live inside the consequences. My legs feel wrong below the knee in that way they do when a man's blood has gone to live somewhere else temporarily. I stop at the corner and brace both hands on the cold stone, breathing like I've been running. I have not been running. I have been very, very still.

Back at the shop, I wash my hands in water cold enough to make a stranger of me for a minute. It helps. Not much. I set tools in order as if order could be contagious. The kettle clatters onto the ring. The stove ticks. Somewhere at the dark edge of town, a fox barks once, neat as a nail tapped home.

I think of the common and the kind of night that asks you to choose between careful and deliberate and rewards you either way if you're honest.

I do not plan to be sensible tonight. I plan to be deliberate.

Every instinct I own is pointed at the common as the light bleeds out of the sky. My body is a tuning fork, humming to a note only two people can hear. Want is an honest tool. Care is the handle. I will use both.

And if the fire throws sparks, I'll catch them before they land where they shouldn't—unless she asks me to let one burn.

Chapter 7 — Embers & Edges
Samantha's POV

By dusk the common at the edge of town is a black bowl filled with breath and expectation. A ring of stones ribs the earth where the bonfire waits—stacked logs and kindling in a careful teepee, peat bricks tucked in like secret grants of heat. People gather in a loose circle, lanterns bobbing, voices low the way voices get when a story is about to start.

I arrive with a paper bag of marshmallows, a sleeve of chocolate-dipped digestives, and nerves that fizz like I've swallowed sherbet and stars. My scarf is wound high; my coat is just this side of sensible. The fox knocker winked at me on my way out like a bad influence—not literal—close enough. I told it to behave. It did not.

Ethan is easy to find. Not because he's loud—he isn't—but because my body seems to have learned his silhouette like a new alphabet overnight. He stands beside the stacked wood speaking with Hamish, one palm braced on a log, sleeves shoved to his forearms. The firelight hasn't started, but somehow there's already a light on him—lanterns, the sky, my traitor attention.

When he looks up, the noise of the common detunes, then sharpens, like the band is checking itself. I lift the paper bag and wiggle it in greeting. He meets me halfway.

"Tribute?" he asks, mouth trying not to smile and failing.

"I hear the geese work night shifts now," I say. "I'm bribing anything with a beak."

"Wise." His gaze flicks to my hands, then my face, then away, as if cataloguing the places I'm warm so he can keep them that way. "You cold?"

"Not yet," I lie, because the edge of the dark has ideas about my bones that my coat isn't entirely arguing with.

He peels his jacket off without making a speech and settles it over my shoulders. "Say when," he murmurs at my collar. "Now," I say, and let the weight settle. It smells like cedar and iron and him. The weight is startlingly intimate, like a palm settling between my shoulder blades—permission, protection, not possession. My fingers find the lapels and hold.

"I'm not carrying you home if you freeze," he says, deadpan, which is code for please keep yourself alive. "I'll truss you to the sledge and drag you."

"Romance lives," I murmur into the collar, not trusting my voice with gratitude.

The kirk bell gives a single, deliberate note. Old Mr. Fergus steps forward with his brass tinderbox, and the town hushes. He strikes flint; sparks kiss the tinder; someone breathes yes for everyone; and then the first lick of flame tongues up through the kindling, curious and sure. The pile gives a soft whoomph, like a creature waking—not literal—close enough.

The fire takes greedily. It always does. Dry sticks crack, peat sighs into heat, and suddenly the black bowl of the common is a place with a sun in it. The town shimmies back to a safe ring. Faces turn gold; shadows get teeth. A cheer rolls around the circle, hearty and relieved, as if we've conjured summer out of October's pocket and gotten away with it.

We drift closer, part of the river of bodies, close enough that my hip brushes Ethan's thigh every time someone behind us jostles. I could step away. I do not. He doesn't make a show of guarding me from the sparks, but he angles his body so that the tiny flecks of fire lift and veer around us like they've been given instructions.

"Bonfires are living," he says, as if replying to a thought I didn't name. His voice is low enough that it's only for me. "You don't bully them. You talk and you listen, and you feed them slow."

"Like code," I say before I can stop myself. "Push too hard and something breaks. Treat it like a conversation, it sings."

He slants me a look that warms in the firelight. "Aye."

The band starts up somewhere behind us—fiddle, whistle, a drum thumped by someone who believes in rhythm like other people believe in saints. Children run with long sticks and toasted marshmallows at the tip like soft moons. The night breathes peat and sugar and the sharpness of first cold.

I pull the bag open and wave it under Ethan's nose. "Payment for last night's lantern chivalry."

"I told you that was self-interest." But he takes one, slides it onto a twig with practised neatness. The sight of a man's hands doing small, careful work shouldn't feel the way it does. It does.

He offers me the twig, and we hold it together, our fingers touching along the stripped bark. The marshmallow turns to glass, then gold, then puffs and blisters. When a tiny tongue of flame catches the edge, I panic and blow; Ethan laughs and shields it with his palm and a little lift of his body, so the wind won't snatch it.

"You hover," I accuse.

"I mend," he corrects, eyes on the sugar. "For future reference, hovering is when you flap. This is steering."

"Steer away," I say, but my voice is warm, not warning.

We slide the marshmallow between two biscuits, chocolate going soft in a rush of heat. When I bite, it strings itself into white silk. A smear lands at the corner of my mouth. Of course it does. The universe is a hacky comedian with excellent timing.

Ethan sees it. For a half-breath, his gaze drops and darkens. The fire pops, bright as a dare.

He could touch me. He could press a thumb to the sweetness and take it—the world organised exactly so that it would be easy. He doesn't. He reaches into his pocket, pulls a clean handkerchief (yes, again), and offers it wordlessly.

Something in me lifts its head and pays attention. This is a man who wants and knows he wants. This is also a man who will not take the shortcut and risk the house. The wanting doesn't go away. It gets sharper. It becomes—God help me—trust.

"Deliberate," I say softly, and he hears everything I'm thanking him for inside the word.

He swallows. "Aye."

A gust yanks at the fire, spins sparks sideways. One lands on my cuff and flashes to a tiny red eye. Before I can react, his hand closes over my wrist—firm but not bruising—and he pinches the ember out, a quick sure press. Heat flares along my skin where he touched. When he lets go, he doesn't step back. His thumb stays for a second longer than necessary, like he's taking a pulse in a story where pulse matters. My pulse taps against his thumb, brazen.

"You all right?" he asks.

"Better than," I say honestly.

The circle tightens and loosens with the music. People lean and sway and fall against one another in happy accidents. Morag passes with a tin of shortbread and a look that says I'll mind the world; you mind each other. Mrs. Baxter patrols like a benevolent hawk. Hamish whoops at the sky and tries to get Katie to reel with him; she swats him and does anyway, the two of them a mess of elbows and joy.

We find a fallen log near the edge of the light and claim it, close enough to the heat to feel it lick our shins, far enough that we can hear ourselves think. Ethan shrugs out of his flannel and lays it across both our knees like we're hiding a secret beneath it. The shared weight is an invented intimacy, ridiculous and devastating.

"Tell me something you haven't told me yet," I say, because the night feels like a jar with the lid off and I want to keep catching its sweetness while it lasts.

He thinks without folding into himself the way guarded people do when asked for softness. He looks into the fire as if it's a person he respects. "When I was a boy," he says, "Da used to bring me to the lamplit dances. Said it was good for a lad to see how a village holds itself together. He'd point out the ones who always had a hand free to catch somebody. He'd nod to them and say, 'That one. Be like that.'" His mouth lifts. "I try."

My throat goes hot. "You succeed," I say, and when he starts to shake his head, I push my knee against his under the flannel. "You do."

He looks at me then—really looks, like a man stepping through a doorway he's planed and hung with his own hands. The breath between us changes temperature. The places we're touching become the only places that exist.

"Your turn," he says, voice roughened.

I watch a column of sparks climb and burn out like tiny brave souls. "I left before I turned myself into someone I wouldn't like," I say. "I was getting smaller for a man who took it as a compliment. I said 'sorry' so much my mouth forgot other shapes. I came here because I wanted a town that told the truth back to me when I told it mine."

He's quiet a moment, long enough that I can hear the crowd and the crackle and the low hiss of peat. When he speaks, it is careful as a hand on a hinge. "Then you're in the right place."

I don't mean to, but my hand goes looking. His meets it halfway like we rehearsed. Fingers fit in that improbable way that makes you believe evolution is romantic when it's not. He doesn't squeeze. He doesn't lace. He simply holds—pressure steady, palm warm and dry, a line between us that says I know where you are.

I don't know how long we sit like that. The fire talks in the old language of wood and wind. The band tosses up a reel and then a soft tune and then a song everyone knows and pretends not to. The stars show up casual and low—so many it feels impolite to stare. Somewhere beyond the common, a fox barks once, neat as a nail tapped home, and the fire tosses up a gout of sparks so exuberant it looks like applause.

Ethan tips his head back, watches the stars, then my face. "Do you feel it?" he asks, a strange, almost shy question for a man like him.

"The heat?" I tease, to buy a heartbeat.

"Aye," he says, faint smile. Then, serious again, "The other thing."

I don't pretend I don't know. The hum that runs under Glenkeld like a cat asleep in sun. The way my candle flares when he passes. The fox knocker's unjustifiable behaviour. The barn lanterns that tiltingly conspired just for us. The way the air seems to collect around his hands like it means to learn them.

"I do," I say, and suddenly I'm not cold at all. "I don't know what to call it."

"Names don't make it more or less true," he says, relief and risk braided through the words.

Sparks leap. One delicate ember drifts toward us. Without thinking, we lift our joined hands, and the ember lands on the back of his knuckles, smoulders, then winks to black. Our joined hands are a small island of gold—twin heat making one steadiness. It should have burned. It didn't. Maybe the skin there is too work-tough to fuss. Maybe the universe patted us on the head and spared the moment. Maybe—and this is where the dangerous thought lives—maybe some things just don't burn if you hold them right.

He turns his hand, studies the faint ash mark, then our fingers. "A seed," he says, so soft I almost think the fire spoke it.

"Aye," I answer, tripping over the accent like a magpie stealing a shiny. He laughs once, low and delighted, and it lights places inside me that haven't seen sun in too long.

The bonfire burns down slow, a big animal getting drowsy. People start to peel away in twos and threes, lanterns bobbing toward lanes and cottage doors. We don't move until the logs slouch, and the heat turns from lover to friend. When we finally stand, my legs have to remember the mechanics of walking without his hand. He doesn't let go right away. Neither do I.

He walks me to the head of Rowan Lane because of course he does. The sky has thinned to a cloth of frost; our breath ghosts. The pumpkins on the low walls have begun to give up their heat to the night, smelling faintly of sugar and earth. My cottage door is a blue rectangle waiting, wreathed in eucalyptus and expectation. The fox knocker is already rehearsing.

"This is where we say goodnight like sane people," I say, standing on my step, his jacket still on my shoulders, his hand still in mine.

"We could go feral," he offers, straight-faced.

"Tempting."

He takes his jacket back inch by inch, shaking the warmth from it and then settling it around his own shoulders like a gentleman who knows how to prolong a parting without being cruel. Our hands slip apart reluctantly. The night seems to lean in to hear what we'll choose.

"Thank you," I say, meaning not just the jacket or the marshmallow lessons or the ember pinched out quick. Meaning the way he didn't snatch sweetness when it was easy. Meaning the way, he steadied the weight without taking it from me. Meaning don't be careful with me; be deliberate.

"Goodnight, Samantha," he says. The way he says my name makes the fox knocker go incandescent with gossip.

"Goodnight, Ethan."

He turns to go, then stops, looks back, and with a small, utterly ruinous certainty, takes my hand and presses it once— firm, measured, like promise given a shape. Not a kiss. Not yet. The first true piece of trust laid on a foundation we've been setting like two patient thieves.

My candle in the window flares with a soft whoomph as he walks away—not literal—close enough.

Chapter 8 — Stormglass

Ethan's POV

The forecast said scattered showers. What we get is a sky splitting itself in two.

It comes down off Ben Carna like a curtain—wind first, shouldering the pines, then rain thick as rope. The first sheet hits the shop's tin roof with a sound like a thousand small hooves, and the gutters choke, and the lane outside goes from cobble to river between one blink and the next.

I'm planing a length of ash and thinking about nothing but grain and edge when the door bangs open and a body blows in with the weather.

Samantha.

She's got her hood up and rain carving her into shine; hair plastered in dark gold at her temple; breath making the air white in front of her. Her coat is losing its argument with the storm. She shoves the door shut with her hip and braces her back against it like she's holding out the sea.

"Hi," she says, absurd and cheerful over the noise. "Your sky is having feelings."

For a second, I just take her in, water running in threads off the point of her nose, her grin a dare at the weather. Then I move—bolt the door, drag an old towel from the peg, get the kettle onto the stove with the speed of a man who knows the order of operations when a person arrives out of breath and bright-eyed at his threshold.

"Come away from that," I tell her, rougher than I mean. "You're standing in a draft that would make saints cuss."

She peels the coat off and it lands on the hooks with a slap. Underneath she's in a knit that's already taken on water, darkening in places I don't look at too long if I want to think straight. She's shivering without admitting it. I take the towel and trap her hands in it, rubbing heat into her fingers like a man trying to start a small emergency fire. "Say when," I murmur. "Now," she manages.

"What possessed you?" I ask, working warmth into each knuckle, each delicate bone.

"Grocery run." Her teeth chitter. "Then the sky decided to flex."

"You could have ducked into Morag's."

"I did. She told me to come here. Said you've better tea and worse sense." She tips a look at the window where rain runs in sheets, the lane now a silver thing pulling towards the burn. "Bridge is a no. Your cabin was a yes."

The word lands between us with the weight of a decision I haven't made aloud. Cabin. My rooms are through the door behind the bench—one big space with a low beam, a hearth, a bed built into a nook, a kitchen that's more shelves than show. I live where I work and work where I breathe. It suits me. It also means there's no way to be casual about letting someone in. You don't bring the weather through that door unless you mean to sit in it.

Her hands finally heat under mine. I should let go. I don't, not yet. "We'll wait it," I say. "Let the burn get over itself. When it drops, I'll get you home."

She glances past me, towards the door that's not just a door. "You're sure?"

I am surer than is safe. "Aye."

The room changes temperature with one word. The shop becomes antechamber. The rain on the roof becomes a curtain, an audience, and a drum.

The kettle makes its soft pre-boil complaint, and we both exhale like we were waiting for a cue. I move first, because motion keeps a man honest. "Towels," I say, because nouns are safe when everything else is a live wire. "Dry things."

I take her through.

My place is small, low-ceilinged, the hearth taking up one wall like a held breath. The stone's cold, but there's tinder, there's kindling, there's the habit of a man who likes to be able to make heat quickly. Shelves line the opposite wall, crowded with the detritus of a life made with hands—boxes I've built to store other boxes, jars with screws sorted by thread, a fox carved in ash sitting on the mantel because it refuses to live anywhere else—not literal—close enough. The rain hushes once removed; the wind lifts and tests the eaves.

She stops just inside, eyes going gentle at the edges. "It looks like you," she says, soft.

"Untidy and hard to heat?" I try, but my chest does an unhelpful thing at the compliment.

"Built to last," she returns, and that's worse.

I busy myself laying the fire. Tinder, kindling, a peat brick. She kneels without asking and adds a twist of shavings she finds in a bowl by the hearth. The white curls catch, give a soft whoomph, and then flame, and the small roar of first heat hits the back of my throat, clean and ancient—not literal—close enough. The room shifts from grey to gold in a handful of breaths.

"Tea," I remind myself, because if I keep looking at her in this light my good sense will become a decorative item. I leave her with the fire and return with the kettle, two mugs, and a clean shirt that will swallow her.

"Turn your back," she says, accepting the shirt and the big towel, eyes dancing because she knows I'm the sort of man who would anyway.

I do, because I am, and because the sound of wet knit sliding over skin is a test I can fail with honour or fail without it. I listen to towel soft against hair, the care she takes with herself. The rain hammers three hard beats on the roof and then breaks into a drumroll. The fire answers in its own language.

"Okay," she says, and there's a thread of shyness under the mischief that makes me brave and tender in the same breath.

I turn. The shirt hangs to mid-thigh; the sleeves are rolled three times. Her hair is a wild, damp crown. The sight twists something low in me and sets it right in the same motion. I hand her tea to buy a second to square myself. She wraps both palms around the mug and breathes the steam like it's a blessing. Our mugs sit side by side on the hearth, twin ribbons of steam making one curl of warmth.

The storm rakes itself down the valley. Light cracks—a white seam—and thunder follows quick on its heels, close enough that the windowpanes tremble. The lights blink once and surrender. The world shrinks to fire, rain, breath.

"Outage," she says, unbothered, and dips her head, a half-smile aimed at the hearth. "We brought our own light—not literal—close enough."

Something wicked and devout curls through me. The fox on the mantel watches like he knows secrets he won't share. I add two more logs. Heat stutters, grows.

"Sit," I say. "Rug's warmer than the chair."

She does, barefoot on the hearthside wool like a sin I'm not allowed to name yet. I take the other corner of the rug opposite her, because if I sit beside her, I won't sit; I'll do something I mean and then every decision afterward will be about living inside that first yes.

We drink. We listen. The storm beats its chest and the fire grins. The space between us is a foot and an ache.

"Tell me," she says, eyes gone steady and dark with reflection and heat. "What do you want?"

She means in the large sense. She also means in the next five minutes. The answer is the same either way.

"Truth," I say. "Work that keeps my hands honest. A roof that doesn't complain in wind. A town that holds. A woman who says what she means and lets me do the same." I tip my mug towards her without smiling. "You?"

"Light," she says, and it should be a joke, but it isn't. "Kindness without the small print. To be wanted with precision." She lifts her mug towards me in a toast I feel down my spine. "To want with it."

I set my drink aside.

We meet in the middle of the rug like two people who've been moving in that direction since the first bunting leaf fell. No lunge. No stumble. Just a controlled slide across a line we drew together.

Up close, she smells like rain in bracken and whatever soap lives in my towel and a note that is only hers. I cup the side of her face and don't hurry, tracing the warm sweep from cheek to jaw with my thumb, mapping the place I didn't take under lanterns. Her eyes close and open and I watch that, too, because watching is part of this—paying attention like it's the first rule.

"Deliberate," she whispers, reminding and inviting.

"Aye," I say.

I don't kiss her. I crowd her with care, palm at the back of her neck, the other at her hip, bringing her into my weather until her knees bump mine and there's no dignified way to pretend we're not choosing. Her breath lands against my throat—warm, a little shaky—and my control shivers like a wire in wind.

She lifts both hands to my chest and presses, not to push away—just to feel. Heat pools low and thick. Her fingers find the seam of my Henley shirt, the hard frame under it, and flex. An honest sound gets out of me.

"Say when," I tell her, not because I'm stopping, but because I want the word when it comes.

She answers by sliding that hand up, palm flat over my heart, then curling to grip the muscle at my shoulder where strength lives. I can feel the shape of her nails through cotton. I can feel the choice, too.

Outside, lightning finds the hill. Thunder rides it down. The fire licks higher, throws heat at our faces and paints us with it. The fox on the mantel tilts his carved head, as if to be sure he's seeing what he's seeing.

"Storm's not passing anytime soon," she says, a thought, a warning, and an excuse offered the way a good host offers bread.

"Good," I say, and put my forehead to hers, relief jerking through me so strong I have to laugh once, low, to bleed it off. "I'm done being sensible."

Her answering laugh is softer, dangerous around the edges. "I like you sensible," she says. "I like you better deliberate."

I let the truth be a gate we both open. My hand on her hip settles, tightens; my thumb draws a slow, thoughtless circle over cotton and heat. Her breath breaks a little on the inhale, and the sight of it takes my body apart and puts it back together with her hands.

We don't kiss. It would be easy, and I don't want easy tonight. I want the kind that writes itself into bone. So I tip my mouth to her cheekbone again, the place I've claimed twice now, and then lower—unhurried—to the hinge of her jaw, the line under her ear, the hollow where pulse lives. Her skin is warm silk stretched over lightning. When I put my mouth there, her pulse jumps against my lip like a small bird deciding to live.

"Ethan," she says, and the way she shapes my name makes me a believer in anything she'd ask.

"Here," I answer, because I am.

Her hands move—at my shoulders, down my back, drawing me closer. The shirt I gave her falls askew, collar slanting; the flash of bare shoulder is a small sunrise that changes the colour of everything. I put my palm there and feel the heat of her like a secret no one has told me I can't keep.

"Say when," I remind, voice gone to gravel.

"Not yet," she breathes, and it does not close a door. It opens every other one.

I pull back enough to see her. Her eyes are blown wide, candlelight caught in them like coins; her mouth is pink and wet where she's bitten it. Pride swells under the want—pride at the steadiness we're choosing, the pace that's ours.

"Stay," I say, and mean the night, the storm, the long after. "Let the burn fall while we teach the fire how to be patient."

She smiles then—small and victorious and soft as the inside of a wrist. "I'll stay."

Another lash of rain hands us its applause. The lights don't even bother trying to come back. The room is only fire and storm and us.

We make tea again because something domestic is the right counterweight to this kind of gravity. We eat the heel of a loaf Morag insisted I take because the woman is a witch of the practical kind. We talk—about nothing and everything; about her first computer, a Frankenstein of spare parts; about my Da teaching me how to read joists like scripture; about the time the geese chased Hamish into the burn, and he pretended he did it for a bet.

And when the talking folds into quiet and the quiet into breath and the breath back into wanting, we go back to the line and toe it like it's a cliff edge we've chosen. I sit with my back to the sofa and she slides between my knees, spine against my chest, the hem of that stolen shirt a problem I plan to solve in a different chapter. My arms come around her without being asked; her head slots under my jaw like the part we made for each other was a real thing and not a story.

The storm rages and then tires; the fire answers and then settles. Somewhere beyond the eaves, a fox barks once, neat as a nail tapped home. At some point the kettle clicks as if it fell asleep sitting up. At some point she drifts and I feel it—the way her breath lengthens, the way her weight gives itself. At some point my chin drops to her hair and I let myself do the thing I haven't in too long: rest with another heartbeat touching mine.

The burn will fall. The bridge will stop sulking. The fox on the mantel will go back to being wood in the morning.

For now, there's this: rain blistering the night, fire being good, a woman folded into me like we both know what we're doing. The storm outside is honest and loud. The one in me is quieter, more dangerous and, for once, I'm not trying to sand it down.

Not yet.

Soon.

Chapter 9 — First Flame
Samantha's POV

The storm has manners at last.

It stops pounding and starts murmuring, the rain thinning to a soft smirr that strokes the windows instead of throwing itself at them. The hearth's gone from roar to glow. The little fox on Ethan's mantel watches the room like a sentry carved from a story. Somewhere in the dark, the burn sulks itself back between its banks with a grudging hiss.

I'm tucked between Ethan's knees on the rug, his chest a warm, solid wall at my back, the hem of his shirt skimming my thighs. I can feel his breath at the crown of my head—steady, deliberate—the way he does everything that matters. The cabin smells like peat and wet wool and tea, and underneath that, his skin: cedar, iron, and something clean that makes my shoulders drop as if told they can rest.

"Tell me when you're cold," he murmurs, the burr of his voice catching at the edges of my spine.

"I will." I tilt my head against his shoulder, letting the weight of this—of us—sink into the floorboards. "But I'm not."

A coal pops, flinging a tiny comet into the air. It arcs, winks out before landing, and I don't know why the sight makes my heart climb into my mouth, except that tonight everything feels like a sign in a language I only half remember.

The fox on the mantel tilts its carved head a fraction. I swear it does—not literal—close enough—and it makes me smile at nothing, at everything.

Ethan's arms skim closer, not trapping, just offering. I let myself lean. The sound he makes is small and low, a small grateful sound that feels like when you fit the last piece into a puzzle and the whole picture settles into place. The storm breathes; the cabin answers. Somewhere beyond the roof, the town gathers itself tight and kind, lanterns asleep in their jars like moths that chose to stay.

"Deliberate," I say, because it's a promise and a spell both.

"Aye." His mouth is near my ear now. I can hear the shape of the word against my skin.

I turn.

Not all the way. Just enough to bring my cheek against his beard, to put my mouth where his jaw is warm and human and absurdly dear. He goes very still, the kind of stillness you make when a bird has decided you're a tree. The fire gives a soft whoomph, taking a breath for us—not literal—close enough.

"Ethan," I whisper, tasting his name as if it's new and sweet and dangerous. "I'm going to kiss you now."

The carefulness in him flares, not to stop me but to meet me with equal weight. "Aye," he says again—permission, agreement, hunger folded inside a single syllable.

I shift to my knees and turn fully, facing him. The shirt slides higher on my thighs; his eyes register it and promptly behave themselves by coming back to my face. The effort wrecks me in the best way. His hands find my waist—not pulling, not pushing—just there, and the heat of them burns through cotton like a secret.

"Hello," I say, because if I don't, I'll forget how to speak and go straight to prayer.

"Hello, sunshine," he answers, and the endearment lands where my sternum lives and lights a candle.

I kiss him.

Tentative, first. A question set softly on his mouth. He answers with a gentleness that unthreads me: the faintest pressure, the warmth of him, the way he doesn't surge, doesn't seize, just meets me and lets me choose the next inch. The taste is smoke and tea and something like heather in low sun. I could live here. I do live here, for one lifted heartbeat.

Then the storm drops a long roll of thunder down the glen, the floor shivers—barely—and something inside me that's been braced for too long finally, finally lets go.

I lean in. He does too, like we agreed a long time ago and only now remembered. The kiss deepens, careful breaking into hunger, a slow catch fire. His hand comes up to cradle the back of my head, fingers slipping into damp hair, anchoring, asking. I open for him like a door that wanted to be open all along. The sound he makes against my mouth—God—goes through me like a struck string.

Everything narrows to heat and breath and the rhythm we find in a handful of seconds: meet, taste, draw back, find again. The world doesn't vanish; it pulls closer—the rain hushing, the hearth gilding the edges of us, the fox keeping watch with carved amusement. The cabin holds while we unravel and reweave.

"Sam," he says into the corner of my mouth, voice equal parts reverent and ruined. My name. His voice. A new frequency I didn't know I could hear.

I want to climb into him, to wear his steadiness like a borrowed coat. I want to be nothing but nerve endings and yes. I reign myself by a thread and move slow. My hands learn him: the bracket of his shoulders, the honest line of scar along a forearm, the heat at the hinge of his jaw, the hollow just beneath his lower lip where a man's care lives. He lets me, breath catching, a quiet "Christ, lass," breaking free when my thumb grazes the notch of his throat.

"Deliberate," I remind, though I sound like I've forgotten the meaning of the word.

"I am," he says, and proves it by kissing me like a craftsman: attention in every pass, patience at the edges, a reverence for good materials. He surprises me—often, exactly right. A teasing brush, a firmer claim, the retreat that makes the return knock the breath out of me. When I make a sound I don't recognize, he answers without questions, without hurry, finding that sound again like he's tuned to it.

The candle on the table stutters and leaps; their light overlaps in a spill of gold—twin flames making one pool of gold. The shadow of the fox stretches long and sly across the far wall. In the grate, an ember brightens into a soft heart and holds—not literal—close enough. I laugh into his mouth, helpless and high on it.

"What?" he murmurs, lips barely leaving mine.

"The room approves—not literal—close enough," I whisper. "The fox is smirking."

"He's judged me since I carved him," Ethan says, not stopping the kiss, just threading the words through it like a ribbon. "Let him blether."

"Blether," I echo, and he smiles against me, and the smile is a kiss all its own.

I shift closer on the rug and the shirt—his shirt—slides off one shoulder. His breath trips. He gets a hand under the collar and sets the fabric right, which feels like contradiction and care until his thumb stays at the curve of bone and rests there, warm and claiming. My pulse taps against his thumb, brazen, and I forget the word for fabric entirely.

"Tell me," he says, voice rough hewn, "if I need to slow."

"You'll know," I say, and mean it. He will. He does. When I push, he yields; when I yield, he fills; when I go still to feel, he holds the stillness like it's holy.

Outside, wind runs an appreciative hand down the eaves and keeps going. The storm, merciful, gives us a pocket the size of this room and a time that feels stolen and earned in the same breath.

I climb into his lap.

Not a pounce. A settling. "Say when," he breathes.

"Closer," I say. Coorie in, the way you do when you find the warm corner of a sofa and a blanket that doesn't scratch. His hands slide to my hips, fingers spanning heat; the quiet growl he bites back sets my nerves alight in neat rows. I kiss him again and again until my lips are slick and my breath is a study in surrender.

Ethan drops his forehead to mine, steadies us both. "You're going to make me forget how to think," he says, and I can hear the smile he can't quite carry.

"That's the idea," I breathe, though the truth is I feel clearer than I have in months—like someone opened all the windows in me and the air's different now.

He kisses a path along my cheek to the corner of my mouth, then lower, along my jaw, to the place he found last night—the one that unmade me neatly—and I gasp, honest and unashamed. The fox on the mantel definitely winks this time. The candle flame lifts like it's trying to see better—not literal—close enough.

"Ethan," I say again, for no reason except that the name does good things to both of us.

"Aye," he answers, and his hands tighten a fraction, pulling me closer, teaching me a new geography of balance and need.

We break for breath and the look on his face is a lesson I wish I'd learned sooner: want without apology, care without caution tape, a man choosing and thinking and somehow making those the same action.

A gust rattles the latch. Somewhere up the brae, a fox barks once, neat as a nail tapped home. The lights—forgotten—make a half-hearted attempt at returning and give up. I laugh, a little giddy. "Your town's in on it."

"Let them," he says, and kisses me like the town can witness, the moon can take notes and he'll still make this a private sacrament.

I answer with my whole mouth.

Tentative is a memory now, sweet and honoured; hunger is the language we're learning quick and well. I taste cinnamon from a biscuit crumb, smoke from the peat, the hum of his restraint giving me the best kind of edge. When I slide my hands under his Henley, the heat of his skin makes me dizzy. He's carved from work and winter mornings, solid and known to himself, and when I skim my palms over that honesty, his head tips back, eyes shut, throat bared like an oath.

"Mo chridhe," he says, not meaning to, I think, and my heart does a startled somersault because even my university-level Duolingo knows my heart when it hears it. The spark that's lived in my belly since I got off the bus flares bright and sure.

"Say it again," I ask, greedy and softer than I mean to be.

He does and follows it with my name like he's carved it with a sharp knife into something built to last.

The storm sighs itself towards the sea. The hearth puts off the sort of heat that makes the air taste like apples and iron. The fox looks insufferably pleased. I feel raw and new and like myself down to the quick.

I kiss him once more, slow, reverent, the way you taste the first bite of something you made with your own hands and waited for properly. He answers with that same reverence, and when we part, our foreheads stay together because it would be rude to rush anywhere else.

"Stay," he says again, not a question this time, but not a command either. A plan spoken in present tense.

"Yes," I whisper. "Stay."

His smile is small and devastating. "Good."

He stands, bringing me with him, easy as lifting a child, except there's nothing innocent about the way my arms wind his neck or the way his hands fit the back of my thighs. The room tilts. The bed in the nook is a shadow and a promise draped in a tartan throw. The candle on the table stretches its flame with a soft whoomph, as if blessing us. In the grate, the soft heart of ember brightens once, like a vow signed in coal—not literal—close enough.

"Deliberate," I say, last reminder and first invitation.

He kisses my temple. "Aye, sunshine." His breath is warm at my ear. "I'll mind the fire."

We go together, slow and sure, autumn at our backs like a chorus—lanterns and pumpkins and the kind of wind that makes leaves let go at last. Outside, Scotland keeps her own counsel. Inside, we write one.

What began as shelter from the storm becomes something else entirely—bigger, older, brighter. And when I finally taste the sound he made when I first kissed him, it's like standing in the doorway of a house that was always mine and finding the lights left on for me.

The fox approves.

So do I.

Chapter 10 — Hearth fire

Ethan's POV

There's a moment between the rug and the bed where the world asks if you mean it.

I do.

She's in my arms—light the way flame is light, not the way feathers are—and the cabin is all pulse and hush. The storm has gentled to a smirr, a cat's-paw against the panes. The hearth has gathered itself and roars soft and low, a big creature happy to be fed. The fox on the mantel pretends not to watch and absolutely watches.

"Deliberate," she reminds, mouth at my temple like a vow. Her breath is warm; her voice is steadier than mine.

"Aye." I lower her to the bed I built with my own hands, the one that fits the nook so tight a careless man might bark his knuckles. I do not bark my knuckles. I have no room in me for clumsiness.

She settles into the tartan like a secret laid where it belongs, my shirt skimming her thighs, hair a damp halo gone unruly with storm. The sight hits me in the ribs—beauty that's taken off its shoes and said it'll be staying a while.

"Come here," she says, not a question, and every old ache steps back to make room for the new good one.

I kneel on the edge, hands braced in the quilt's weave, and let myself look. Want is honest. So is reverence. Between them there's a path a man can walk without losing his name.

"Tell me if I go wrong," I say, rough because care makes me that way.

"You won't," she answers, and—God—trust lands heavier than any hunger.

I take my time. I learn the map laid out for me in the soft gold of the fire. The curve of her cheek, the corner of her mouth where laughter lives, the line of throat to collarbone that undid my good sense hours ago and makes a liar of restraint now. My hands are callused; I use them gently. My mouth knows craft; I use it slow. When I draw a line with my lips to the place beneath her ear, her breath breaks on the inhale, and the sound lights me from the inside like a struck match.

"Ethan." My name again, the way she says it making a house out of bone.

"I'm here." I am, in all the ways that matter.

The kiss deepens, careful breaking into hunger, a slow catch fire. I taste smoke and honey and the sound she makes when I get it right. She opens for me and I meet her there—no hurry, no taking without asking—just pressure and answer, the rhythm we've been finding all night.

Outside, wind steps down from the roof. The light in the cottage holds steady. The fox, insufferable creature, seems to smile into the room's heat and get away with it—not literal—close enough.

"Look at me," she whispers, when I would bury my face in the place that makes breath into pleading. I do. Her eyes are dark and wide, candlelight caught in them like coin. "I want to see you choosing me."

I didn't know I needed the words until she gave them. "Aye," I say, and choose again, and again, until choice isn't a cliff but a door swinging true on hinges I've set, planed, and hung.

The first time we find the same place at once, the hearth throws a soft whoomph—a pleased beast rolling in its own warmth—and the ember in the grate rounds itself into a small, perfect heart. I don't believe in outward signs. I do believe in rooms that learn their people. This one approves.

She laughs, breathless, forehead to mine. "Your house is very supportive."

"He's a gossip," I say, which is insane, calling a room a he, but there's no court to fine me in this weather. "He'll tell the woodpile."

"Let him." She kisses me quick for wickedness, slow for kindness, and then thorough because she is, and the world turns on that.

We find a rhythm.

It isn't showy. It isn't the kind of thing a man boasts of in pub corners. It's the oldest pattern under all our other making: touch and be touched, give and be given, hold and be held. There are hands everywhere and never in a hurry, mouths learning each other's language quickly and well, small sounds neither of us has made in too long and have missed like fresh bread. When I lose the thread, her palm finds my jaw and sets it. When she goes quiet to listen to her own body, I get quiet too and learn what silence is for.

"Good?" I check, because the word has work to do tonight.

"God, yes." She laughs into the back of her hand, wrecked and shining. "I didn't know I could feel…" She shakes her head, incapable of finishing, which is a mercy, because I'd like to be the one who makes finishing difficult for her, often.

I let myself look again, openly, like a man at his own wedding to a life he built and thought might not hold. Joy is a dangerous thing to carry. It makes a soft target of your chest. I carry it anyway.

"Mo chridhe," I say, not careful now, and watch the word land where words matter. She hears it; of course she does. She pulls me down and says my name like an answer to it.

"Say when," I murmur against her mouth.

"Not yet," she breathes, and I smile into the kiss because that's my favourite prayer.

Cloth shifts. I learn her by hand and by mouth—jaw, throat, the warm line to collarbone—until breath turns to pleading. When I push my shirt higher on her thighs, heat climbs my wrist like a secret. She arches; I mind the fire. I take my time. I use my hands the way I use my tools: sure, steady, listening. The sound she makes when I find the place that sings—aye—that'll live in my bones.

She asks for more and I give it; when I ask, she answers with a lift of her hips and a yes that lands in my palm. I hold the pace we set together, slow until it isn't, then slower again at the edge.

"Look at me," she says when I'd hide my face in the place that turns breath to prayer. I do. Candlelight coins her eyes. She watches me choose her, and choosing turns into moving, turns into the clean, right slide of home.

"Christ," I manage, wrecked and grateful. "You feel—" Words fail. Care doesn't. I keep it deliberate: each stroke a promise kept, my hand sure at the small of her back, her nails a map across my shoulders.

The room narrows to heat and honest breath, the old boards keeping our secret while we learn each other properly. When I feel her body gather, I say it again—"Say when"—and her yes breaks open the night. I follow close after, not because I can't help it but because I choose to, and the choice makes the falling clean.

When we finally tip over together—heat taking us, breath going wild, both of us undone and remade in the same startled second—the candle on the table lifts its flame with a soft whoomph, straight and tall like a boy in church who's decided to behave—not literal—close enough, and the fox approves with a grin carved thirty months ago that looks made for now.

"Hi," she says into the hollow where my collarbone meets, a shy greeting for the part of the night that starts when sense returns. "Still here?"

"Aye." I turn and kiss her hair, damp again but with different weather. "Not moving unless the house falls down."

"It won't." She taps the beam above us, fond. "You built it."

We lie sideways in the warmth, tracing nothing thoughts. She tells me about a teacher who smuggled old PCs out of a skip so kids could take them apart; I tell her about Da teaching me to listen to studs behind plaster, the way a wall tells you where it holds its secrets. She laughs when I attempt an American accent and says my 'r's are a war crime. I teach her coorie and she rolls it around in her mouth until it becomes something any Scottish granny would approve of. We decide that tea is required and then do not move for five more minutes because the kitten-soft weight of the quilt and the rhythm of two hearts is a narcotic a man would be a fool to kick.

Eventually I untangle, set the kettle, bank the fire for a second wind. The cottage's night noises come back like shy neighbours—rafters settling, the wee scratch of a mouse reconsidering rent, rain finishing its last story on the sill. I bring tea, I bring the heel of a loaf with butter and honey, because Morag's influence is a presence even when she's nowhere near. Samantha sits up against the headboard, my shirt a lost cause, tartan a flag of surrender, cheeks pinked from heat and from being looked at like this by a man lately taught he's allowed to look.

"Don't move," I say, and she freezes, alarmed. I shake my head. "Not—Christ, no—don't move because I'm going to remember this until I can't."

She softens, then smiles, and it kills me dead and brings me back better. "Then remember it properly," she says, tipping her chin, proud and unashamed, mine to look at, and I do, with the reverence you give a sky right before snow.

We eat like ordinary folk, fingers sticky with honey, butter melting to our wrists. We trade the mug back and forth and argue lightly about how much sugar tea deserves. (None, I say; three grains, she says; we compromise at ridiculous and I pretend to be offended.) She steals my slice of bread. I let her and steal a kiss instead, which she calls a fair trade and I call daylight robbery. She tells me the fox is definitely smirking now. I inform her he was carved with that face and there's a limit to what a lad can do with a chisel.

"Make me a promise," she says when we've done the ridiculous domestic bit that makes everything before and after more real.

"If I can keep it."

"Keep this deliberate," she says. "Even when it's easy. Especially then."

I consider the fire—the way it gives most when you feed it measured, steady, without throwing the whole woodpile on for the crackle. I consider the house that holds because I set the bones true when I built it. I consider the sharpness in me I've spent years learning to sheath. I consider the woman whose yes made my name heavier on my tongue in the best way.

"Aye," I say. "I'll mind the fire."

She presses her forehead to mine, breath warm, tea and honey, and I feel the promise take not just in my mouth but in whatever part of a man measures his life in inches of goodness. Somewhere outside, a fox barks once, neat as a nail tapped home.

We drift again, not into sleep straight away, but into that sweet in-between where bodies cool and heat in turns and the night makes a bowl of itself and says coorie in, the worst of it's past. I pull the quilt higher when her shoulder pebbles; she tucks toes under my calf and pretends she isn't. The kettle clicks for no reason anyone human can hear, as if adjusting its memory of boiling.

"Tomorrow," she says, words half-melted, "pumpkin carving in the square. I'll beat you."

"You won't," I say at once because some things are sacred. "But I'll tidy your mess and call it art."

She laughs, gone to feathers, and falls asleep against me, mouth parted a little, lashes making shadows I could live in. I stay awake longer than I should, because even a sensible man gets to keep watch the first night his house learns a new name for quiet.

When I do sleep, it's hard and clean. No old dreams. No doors slammed. No hands empty. Just the crack of settling timber and the soft breath of a woman who asked me to choose and watched me do it.

If there's magic, I don't need it named. The candle burns down in perfect calm, the ember in the grate holds its wee heart-shape as if to say 'aye, that'—not literal—close enough until morning, and the fox—smug bastard—keeps smiling like he knew the ending and is pleased we took the long way anyway.

Chapter 11 — Morning Honey
Samantha's POV

I wake to the sound of rain remembering how to be quiet.

Light sifts through the cabin's small window the way flour falls through a sieve—soft, slow, dusting everything in gentle. The hearth is a glow instead of a roar; the peat has settled into itself like a cat after mischief. Somewhere in the walls, the cottage makes the tiny, contented noises of old timber that slept well. I stretch and discover I'm already smiling, which feels like the sort of miracle you don't name in case it gets shy.

Ethan is a warm line at my back, breath steady where the crown of my head finds his throat. One of his hands has gone thoughtful in the night and found my waist. When I shift, his palm flexes—hello—and then settles, not possessive, exactly, just sure. I tuck myself closer with a small, greedy, coorie, and feel him huff a laugh into my hair.

"Morning, sunshine," he says, voice hoarse with sleep and something else that coils low in me like a satisfied fox.

"Morning," I answer, and the word comes out as honey.

We don't rush it. The room is its own spell and we're not fools. We lie there and let the day assemble itself around us: the kettle remembering it exists, the wind testing the eaves, a distant smirr that has gone from siege to blessing. The fox on the mantel—insufferable—appears to be smirking at the ceiling—not literal—close enough.

"Tea," Ethan murmurs, not moving, like a man conducting a risk assessment between comfort and kettle.

"Please," I say, not moving either, like a woman bold enough to ask for both.

He kisses the place behind my ear in lieu of a promise and disentangles with that particular patience I've already learned is just how he is with anything worth keeping. Watching him pull on yesterday's Henley should not feel like a religious experience. It does. When he stands to bank the fire and set the kettle, the cabin shifts around him the way a room rearranges itself to better suit a favourite chair.

"Don't look at me like that," he says without turning, amused and a little undone.

"Like what?" I pat the quilt into order, which is to say disarray, because quilts have willpower of their own.

"Like you've decided to keep me," he says, soft enough that the peat might keep the confession for us.

I prop myself on an elbow and let him see me decide for a beat. "Aye," I say, practicing my local. "I reckon I have."

The sound he makes is low, unsteady and has my name in it without saying it. The kettle chooses that moment to boil as if offended by sentiment. He pours. When he brings me a mug, his thumb grazes my wrist like punctuation. My whole body reads the sentence correctly.

We drink in the quiet that belongs to people who did not sleep alone and are better for it. He steals a kiss between sips; I steal his mug and his breath. The candle on the table lifts its flame with a soft whoomph as if taking attendance and then settles, pleased—not literal—close enough. Our mugs sit side by side, twin ribbons of steam making one curl of warmth. When I swing my legs out of bed, the hem of his shirt kisses my thighs and his pupils commit crimes.

There's a faint pink on my jaw in the shape of his beard. I touch it and raise an eyebrow. He goes redder than a rowan berry and mutters something about "craft marks," which makes me laugh so hard I have to set the tea down before I commit a spill.

"Breakfast," he declares, escaping to dignity via domesticity. "Or the town'll find us face-down at the market and blame Morag for feeding us poetry and nothing else."

He moves around the tiny kitchen like the house taught him its choreography. I pad across the rug and help myself to the drawer with cutlery; it fits my hand as if it were expecting me. We assemble oatcakes and eggs and a scandalous amount of butter. He lifts me by the hips to sit on the counter so I can reach the good jam at the back of the top shelf. "Say when," he murmurs. "Now," I breathe. I make a sound I didn't intend to make; he pretends to be a gentleman and is, and also isn't, and the eggs do not burn because he is a man who can multitask when properly motivated.

We eat at the little table with our knees knocking. He tells me Mrs. Baxter's sheep have a jailbreak rate that rivals petty criminals; I tell him about the first bit of code I wrote that solved a problem nobody else admitted was there. We trade bites. We trade looks. The fox keeps score and declares us both winners.

By the time the plates are rinsed and stacked, the rain has thinned to a polite drizzle. Glenkeld's day hum rises outside, the square already finding its market voice: clink of jars, flap of canvas, someone scolding a spaniel who is not sorry. We stand at the door we fixed together last night. He leans one hand to the frame; I lean the opposite; it feels like a private handshake with the house.

"Walk in with me?" he asks, simple as a nail set true.

"Try and stop me." I slide into my boots, steal his scarf because it smells like him, and tuck my hair under my beanie. At the threshold, he touches the fox knocker with two knuckles like it's a talisman and then—deliberate, always—presses a kiss to my temple that lands like a vow you don't have to say out loud yet.

The lane is washed clean, cobbles shining like the town got a fresh coat of truth overnight. Pumpkins sit smug, fat with rain, their stems wearing drops like jewellery. We start towards the square and the world conspires to make it all a little too on the nose in ways that make me giddy: a single bunting leaf lets go and rides the air into my palm; the geese at Muir's far-off fence honk in what I will be calling approval; a cat stretches on a windowsill and blinks at us like we are a soap opera it's been enjoying. Somewhere up the brae, a fox barks once, neat as a nail tapped home.

"Good omen," I say, palming the leaf as if it matters.

"Name it and it's twice true," Ethan says, and for a ridiculous, perfect second I imagine him saying that about other things, bigger things, and my heart executes a flourish.

Glenkeld does what Glenkeld does best: makes a bustle of itself. Morag's bookshop door is propped, a bell tied with ribbon, so the chime is more celebration than warning. She spots us and lifts her eyebrows so high I'm surprised they don't escape her face. Then she arranges her expression into a welcome so sincere, I could eat it with a spoon.

"Morning, hen!" she sings, sliding a paper bag across the counter before we've even crossed the threshold. "For your troubles."

"What troubles?" Ethan mutters, failing to hide a smile.

"The kind that leave a lass with honey on her mouth," Morag says, eyes twinkling as if she invented innuendo. She leans over. "And a gentleman with a neck that says he slept badly on account of good reasons." She tuts, delighted, and shoos us out with a pair of cinnamon doughnuts and zero shame. "Off with ye. The market wants witnesses."

We make it five steps before Hamish intercepts, all grin and scandal. "I'm no' sayin' the geese were gossipin' at dawn," he says, looping an arm around Ethan's shoulders, "but there was honkin' from the hedges that sounded like applause."

"Get tae," Ethan tells him, which I translate broadly as 'please perish.'

"Afternoon, Samantha," Hamish adds, turning gallantry up to eleven. "Ye look radiant. That's either the Highland air, or my brother's finally usin' his head for something other than holdin' his hat."

"Both," I say sweetly, and Ethan groans and nudges him with older-brother fond violence. Hamish winks at me and drifts away like a bard who knows when he's landed the line.

The market is full: apples in wooden crates, skeins of wool like sugared sherbet, jars of honey that hold their own weather. Children queue for face painting; a boy emerges with a very serious fox on his cheek and salutes me with his oatcake. The apiarist's stall glows; the blacksmith's anvil rings; the pie lady's wares steam in a way that makes me consider proposing to a crust.

We fall into the rhythm of it: browsing, gossiping, being given things we absolutely try to pay for and absolutely are not allowed to. Every glance we share is a string pulled between last night and now, taut and sparking. Nothing showy; no spectacle. Just the quiet miracle of having been inside someone's arms and then standing beside them like that secret is the finest armour.

At the pumpkin stall, a sign advertises this afternoon's carving contest in a hand that understands flourish. "Ach, there ye are," the vendor says. "We've a slot with your names on it."

Ethan tilts his head at me. "Do you have the courage to be humbled, engineer?"

"By a man who thinks character trumps symmetry?" I pinch his side through flannel and feel his laugh under my fingers. "I'll carve a masterpiece and then deploy it before your candle goes in."

"Threats," he murmurs, pleased beyond reason. "Dangerous."

"Flirtation," I correct, equally pleased. "Also, dangerous."

We pay our entry like honest citizens and accept our numbered tokens. Passing the baker, I tug Ethan to a stop. "Tell me something true," I say, slipping us into the shadowed edge of a canvas awning where the world feels quieter.

He leans a shoulder to the post and considers, trying to give me the good stuff and not the easy. I wait, because patience is my new party trick.

"I keep wanting to put my hand at the small of your back," he says finally, low, eyes on my mouth. "Every time a crowd presses, every time a cart rattles near, every time the wind decides to change its mind. Even when there's no need. I keep not doing it, because I won't take what I haven't been given." His mouth shifts. "That's the truth."

My insides fold and refold like warm dough.

So, I take his hand, turn, and set it exactly where his truth asked for. "There," I say, breath skating its edge. "Given."

His inhale is a beautiful, wrecked thing. He doesn't pull me in, but his fingers curve as if the town just aligned all its streets to us. "Aye," he says. "Good."

We resume our loop like adults who have not just quietly rearranged gravity. People nod, and nobody stares. Mrs. Baxter inspects our lanterns (imaginary), approves our posture (I'm certain), and informs Ethan that the fence he fixed has held against both sheep and a gale, which I suspect is code for 'I see you, son, and so does the rest of the village'. He bears it with stoicism. I grin until my face aches.

By mid afternoon, the sky has lifted to a pale blue that feels like a fresh page. We stake out a table for carving under a string of paper moons. A teenager in fingerless gloves hands out blunt knives with the solemnity of a coronation.

"Rules," he intones. "No blood. No swears carved on pumpkins. No likenesses of local officials."

"Who tried that last year?" I whisper.

"Hamish," Ethan and the teen say together, and I snort cider.

We set our gourds on the boards like rivals in a duel—the symmetrical one I picked with pride weeks ago and the lopsided character Ethan chose today with a look that said, 'trust me.' He sketches with a bit of charcoal; I plan like a coder, thinking where the cuts will give most light. Our elbows brush and don't move away.

"Wager?" I ask, carving the first sure slice.

"Name it."

"If I win, you teach me to chisel without takin' my thumb off."

"If I win," he says, eyes all wicked winter and warm hearth, "you let me carry your pumpkin home and choose where we set it."

"Rigged," I accuse. "You get your way either way."

"Aye," he says, unabashed, and then—deliberate—tips his shoulder into mine so lightly anyone else would call it a

Autumn in Glenkeld: Pumpkins & Firelight

bump and I will be thinking about it tonight when candles are lit again.

We cut. We scoop. He pretends not to admire my clean lines; I pretend not to admire the way he coaxes personality from a crooked mouth and a single raised brow. The crowd mills, cheers, laughs at Hamish's heckling. A breeze stirs, and a single paper moon turns to face us like a watcher curious about outcomes. My knife slips once and he's there, big hand steadying mine and the rind both, the touch a simple safety and a brand under my skin.

"Thanks," I say, low.

"Always," he answers, not looking away.

We finish with sticky fingers and orange crescents of rind in our hair. When the judging comes round—Morag, the pie lady and Mrs. Baxter in the world's least impartial tribunal—they award Ethan "Most Character" and me "Cleanest Glow." We bow like it matters and are handed ribbons that might as well be engagement paperwork for how my chest responds.

"Good work," he says in my ear as we gather our spoils. "We'll light them together tonight."

"Deliberate," I remind, because it's our word and because saying it tastes like yes.

We wander home by the long way, hands not quite linked, aura draped in the sort of calm that doesn't fear what comes next. At Rowan Lane, the blue door looks smug; the fox knocker prepares its best wink. We set our pumpkins on the step side by side but unlit, a promise for dusk. He touches my jaw with two fingers where the faint pink mark has deepened in the cold and looks like something he'd fight a dragon to keep from aching.

"Tonight," he says.

"Tonight," I promise, and the candle I left in the cottage—swear to God—flares with a soft whoomph in the window as if it heard us—not literal—close enough.

He kisses my forehead—deliberate always—and steps back into the lane. He only gets halfway to the corner before turning for one more look, one more smile that lands heavy and sweet, one more small, simple 'aye' I can tuck into my pocket and hold when the wind gets above itself.

I lean against the blue door, hand over a heart that's learning a new beat. The town hums like a song I finally know the words to. Inside, the kettle remembers to boil. Outside, leaves let go in their own time.

It's an ordinary day. We sold nothing, bought doughnuts, carved a face, got ribboned by a biased jury. And still—every glance is ember, every brush is spark, and the whole of Glenkeld feels an inch nearer to magic because he keeps setting his hand at the small of my back like the town asked him to, and I said yes.

Chapter 12 — Measure Twice
Ethan's POV

After the market, the town exhales like a horse uncinched.

Canvas comes down in damp flaps. Ribbons clack against their strings. The last of the cider steam blows sideways up the close and disappears. I see her to the mouth of Rowan Lane—blue door a square of sky, fox knocker angling for scandal—not literal—close enough, our two pumpkins sweating rain like contented beasts—and I make myself do the sensible thing: kiss her temple, promise tonight, and turn away before I forget the path that leads back to my own door.

The shop is warmer than it has a right to be at day's end. The stove ticks; the air smells of oil and fresh-cut apple where someone abandoned a core near the vice, likely me. I hang my flannel shirt, roll my sleeves, and try to put the afternoon where it belongs: a good crowd, decent trade, no injuries, one sunshine engineer who laughs like a rope thrown across a gap and pulled tight.

I last nine minutes before I admit I am a lost cause and let the day in.

The bench is an altar for a man who prays with shavings. I clear it down to the gouges and the old glue ghosts. Planes in a row; chisels nested in their rack; square, pencil, marking knife. My hands know the drill. My head, though—my head runs after her like a daft dog every time I set a tool down.

Her fingers warm under mine when her knife slipped. The wee sound she made when I steadied. The way she held my gaze and said there, and I moved there, and the world got small and very exact.

I put my thumb on the pencil and pull a line.

The line is the front edge of a drawer I have not been asked to build.

A shallow one, dovetailed true, to sit flush under a slab that isn't a table yet and already is. Space enough for pencils, for a ribbon with a key, for whatever small thing a woman might keep between near and closer. I write aye in the corner of the scrap and feel like a lad caught doodling a name he likes. I round the letter out with my thumb and scowl at myself so I don't float off the floor.

"Right," I tell the wood, because someone needs telling. "Measure twice."

I cut a test tail for the dovetail out of ash, light and forgiving. The saw's song is a good one—no catch, no complaint. I pare the cheek clean, feel the last whisper of waste come away like breath fog on a winter pane. It fits the practice socket loose—good enough for a dry run, not tight enough for pride. Which is to say, just like me today.

The bell over the door taps once. Morag's silhouette is a story the rafters know.

"I come with neutral carbs and aggressive advice," she says, sliding a paper bag onto the bench. Cardamom finds the air like a hymn. "Which do you want first?"

"Neither," I say, and take both.

She sets a hip to the bench and pretends the dovetail test is the only thing she came to inspect. "That joint's honest," she says. "Mind the knife wall on your pins. And mind your head." She cuts me a look that would proof dough. "You've got the face on."

"What face?"

"The one that says, 'Something good has arrived and must be interrogated for crimes.'" She steals half a knot and my napkin. "Eat. Say out loud whatever you're telling yourself in that stubborn skull."

I chew, because sugar keeps old friends from throwing flour at you. "It's fast," I say finally. "Feels like standing under a roof I set in a day. I've seen roofs I set in a day. I don't fancy picking slate out of anyone's hair."

Morag's mouth gentles, which is a weapon she doesn't use lightly. "Do you remember the first time you planed curl out of oak?"

"Aye."

"You didn't bully it. You didn't leave the iron set for pine and hope. You took light passes and watched the figure appear like a bairn making up its mind about the world." She taps the ash tail. "Deliberate isn't the same as distance."

"I know."

"Do you?" She folds her arms. "Because you MacKinnons are very gifted at disappearing in place and calling it 'care.'"

I deserve that. I hate that I deserve that. "I don't want to nick her," I say, low. "Or me."

"Then don't." Morag leans, soft enough to be kind, sharp enough to count. "Say near and mean it. Say time if you need it and mean that, too. But don't be a ghost at your own bench. It's untidy."

I look at the scrap with aye in the corner and at the first honest tail of a drawer I shouldn't be making yet and feel the old balk loosen its jaw. "Aye," I say. "I hear you."

She leaves me with a second knot, a wink big enough to scandalise the clock, and a bell tap that sounds like a benediction if you squint at it hard enough.

I sweep. I set the tail aside where I'll trip on it later and call that accountability. I open the drawer under the bench, take out the little brass fox I cast last winter on a dare to my own patience, and turn it in my fingers until the metal picks up the heat of my hand. It was meant for nothing in particular. It looks like himself on her blue door, all cheek and witness. I set it on the shelf above the stove where the light catches the curve of its smug wee jaw. "Behave," I tell it. It refuses.

Light dies quick as a spark under an unkind boot this time of year. Dusk and the grey after it push at the windows; the gutter outside starts its dragging complaint as the smirr remembers itself. I bank the stove. I lay out tomorrow's call—hinges for Mrs. Mackie, a note to pick up galvanised staples at the smith, a sketch to remind my hands where the next good line is.

There's still the business of tonight. Two pumpkins at a blue door, unlit on purpose. A promise to make a small spectacle of patience. The thought of her mouth when the match catches. The thought of my own face reflected in her window glass, ridiculous and earnest.

I pick up my jacket. I put it down. I pick it up again because a life can be built out of a man repeating the right verbs until they stay put.

Halfway to the lane, the wind changes its mind and shoulders me back a step. Paper moons clack once in unison like somebody's bones complaining at a reel. Hamish appears at my elbow out of the weather the way brothers do.

"Ye've got the look of a man who's meant to be somewhere and is terrified he'll arrive," he observes, hands stuffed in pockets, grin like a gull that's learned to pick locks.

"Go away," I tell him, without heat.

He falls into step anyway. "You'll be fine. You've been practising this one a while."

"What one?"

"Using your words."

I cut him a look that would fell an ash tree. He grins larger, which is natural selection's way of daring me to evolve.

At Rowan Lane, the blue door looks like it was painted by a man who knew I'd need a landmark one day. Our pumpkins sit fat and expectant. The fox knocker is a menace. The window's candle—hers—throws a little flare with a soft whoomph when we cross the last yard of cobble, as if performing for a critical audience—not literal—close enough.

Hamish peels off with exaggerated casualness and whistles something that died on a fence post in 1987. I stand. I breathe. I lift my hand, and the fox bumps my knuckles because brass is lawless in October.

The door opens before I knock.

She's there with matchbox in hand and a grin that makes my sternum go two sizes too big for the rest of me. My scarf is still at her throat because she stole it and I let her. Her hair is a riot contained by a beanie, nearly. Behind her shoulder the cottage is all lamp and beeswax and the smell of sugar baked into wood.

"Hi," she says, wrecking me with two letters.

"Hi," I say, and it comes out like a plan.

We do the small ceremony in the rain's fine breath: wicks trimmed, match struck, the first catch a soft whoomph that shows up proud and then minding itself—not literal—close enough. Her lantern throws steady light; mine gives a lopsided grin; the circles pool and meet on the stone between our boots and become one long pill of gold—twin light making one pool. She laughs, soft. I don't tell her I've been thinking of that strip of light since the first sketch of a drawer I shouldn't build yet.

We don't kiss. Not here. Not this minute. It's not restraint. It's choosing. We stand in the door's shelter and let the pumpkins do the talking for us: near can be a thing you do with your shoulders touching and your mouths behaving.

My hand finds the back of her jacket at the exact middle where I could put a nail and set a line from plumb to true. (I do not put a nail in my girl. Standards.)

"Tomorrow," she says, voice low. "We'll carve the last of the scraps and eat things Mrs. Baxter calls food and everyone else calls crimes."

"Aye," I say. "And I'll fix Mackie's fence before she takes a broom to me in the square."

She tips her head. The beanie tries to escape. I catch it because I am a gentleman and because she would otherwise bully weather with hair alone. When I set the hat back, I pause with my fingers light at the brim. "Say when," I murmur. "Now," she breathes, and she holds still, welcoming the fuss, and that small trust—let me set this right, in this inch—is a board seating home somewhere I didn't know needed it.

"Walk you in?" I ask, asking for more than one step.

"Tonight, I'm yours at the step," she says, honest, kind. "Tomorrow, soup and scandal. After, we'll see."

"Deliberate," I agree, and the fox knocks the back of my hand with his shadow like he's signing documents.

I make myself leave before I invent a reason not to. Back at the shop, the stove has held its ember the way decent stoves do; the shavings have settled like pale snow that failed to be cold. I put the practice tail where I'll see it in the morning. I write near on the same scrap as aye and blow out the lamp.

Sleep is not tidy. I dream of hinges and a river of oak under glass and a word I say in a small room to a woman in my scarf. I wake twice—once at a gust that wants a new name; once at the thought that speed is a liar and I don't have to hire him.

In the thin light before dawn, I sit up and put a hand to my jaw where her laugh lives. The shop is quiet in that good way, rafters content, fox on the mantel pretending he slept and absolutely lying.

All right, then.

I'll mend what I touch. I'll mind the fire. I'll keep my hand where it belongs and my words ready. When the wind gets up—and she will—I won't go to distance and call it care. I'll say near and time and aye and mean every one.

Measure twice. Cut once. Choose and keep choosing.

Outside, a fox barks once, neat as a nail tapped home. Inside, the ember rounds itself—just for a heartbeat—into that daft wee heart and settles—not literal—close enough.

Chapter 13 — Hairline Cracks

Samantha's POV

The day after ribbons and market laughter arrives dreich and thin, a sky the colour of unwashed wool stretched over Glenkeld. The square puts on its cheer anyway—paper moons tinkling against their strings, the bakery turning out trays of shortbread that smell like good intentions. My cottage holds a warmer weather of its own: last night's candle stub on the table, two pumpkin ribbons hanging from the fox knocker like medals on a rascal.

I code with my feet tucked under me and a mug of tea going cold because I keep re-reading the same line. My brain, usually a tidy tool chest, is a jumbled drawer: last night's stolen kiss in the market's shadow; Ethan's hand steady at the small of my back; the way he said 'real' without saying it. Want and wonder have moved in together, and neither is good at doing the dishes.

At noon, a tap at the pane makes me jump. Hamish, rain-beaded and grinning, holds up a paper bag big enough to house a cat and mouths, 'Morag'. I meet him at the door; the fox knocker winks like it's been paid to—not literal—close enough.

"For the genius," Hamish announces, handing over pastries and a weather report. "Storm's sulking oot to sea, but wind's coming round later. We're shifting hay at the green for the ceilidh tomorrow. You comin'? We'll need brains to tell us where to put the bales so folk don't break their—" he glances at my face and chooses the safe end of the sentence, "—ankles."

"I can project manage hay," I say solemnly.

He leans sideways, peers into my cottage like a magpie looking for mischief to steal. "My brother'll be by about four," he adds, too casual. "Don't let him get lost in his head. He's a champion at it. Gold medals for brooding. We keep them in a box labeled 'numpty'."

"What's wrong?" My chest tightens before my brain can tell it to behave.

"Nothing ye can't fix with a biscuit and the truth," Hamish says cheerfully, which is not the same as nothing, and swings off with a whistle, leaving damp footprints and a shrug.

I tell myself I won't clock-watch.

At four, I fail not to clock-watch.

By five, the streetlamps blink on, making coins of the puddles. I cut the wicks for our pumpkins and nestle candles inside—my clean glow, his crooked grin—match poised. The blue door waits like a polite question. A wind runs a cold finger down the lane and sets the paper moons to a soft clatter.

At five-twenty, I give in and text—the first time, what could go wrong? *You alive or have the geese unionised?* The bubble hangs unsent for one ridiculous heartbeat while my fingers decide whether care is cowardice. I hit send. The ellipsis appears. Disappears. Appears. *Shop ran over. On my way now.*

Relief and something like pre-emptive disappointment get in a shoving match in my chest. I light both pumpkins anyway. Two flames lift with a soft whoomph, like shy greetings—not literal—close enough. Their circles overlap on the wet stone—twin light making one pool of gold.

He arrives ten minutes later with rain on his shoulders and sawdust at his cuffs, a contradiction wrapped in a flannel shirt. He's…different. Not cold. Not unkind. Just drawn around the edges, like a blueprint overlaid with a shadow. His smile is there; it just lands short.

"Sorry," he says, breath fogging. "Baxter's gate came off the post in the gust. Sheep had a look at freedom and decided they liked the view."

"How dare they," I say lightly, holding open the door with my hip. "Come thaw."

Inside, the cottage offers him warmth like a dog offering its favourite toy. He stands just inside it, not quite claiming it, rain steaming off his shoulders, the fox knocker gossiping silently from the latch. When I reach for the buttons of his jacket—habit, intimacy learned in a night—he stills, a small, involuntary 'haud' that isn't a flinch but sits in the same neighbourhood.

I let my hand fall. "Tea?"

"Aye," he says, grateful to the noun. "Please."

The kettle chatters. The cottage breathes. We stand with the table between us, and it should be comfortable—it has been, is—but there's iron filings in the air and I can feel the magnet turn. He tells me about the gate. I tell him about a payment bug that tried to sneak past me and got its tail caught. The words are fine; it's the spaces between them that bring a draft.

"Ethan," I say, when we've both finished being polite. "Did I step on a crack I didn't see?"

His jaw works. He looks at the pumpkins on the step through the window like they might answer for him. "No." Then—honest, because he doesn't know how else to be—"Aye. Not you. Me."

Old story, Morag had said without saying. The leash on temper. The family weight. Not me. Me. I walk around the table because conversation has to be carried, not shouted across. I stand where he can see my hands if he needs to.

"Say it wrong first," I offer. "Then say it right."

He breathes, heavy. "It's fast," he says. "Feels like…like I've set a roof in a day and I'm standing under it before the joists know their job." His mouth twists. "I've been a man who hurt with hurry before. Not with hands. With pulling away. With letting the heat run me and leaving ash after. I can't be that to you." He lifts a hand and lets it fall, helpless. "So, my body says, 'easy now', and my brain says 'aye', and then you look at me like—" He shakes his head, stops short of the precipice of saying too much. "I'm a coward today," he finishes, soft and brutal.

It lands—not like a slap, but like the sharp air of a door opened onto weather. He is not wrong about speed. The truth, however, has sharp corners. I take one breath. Then another.

"Okay," I say, because the first job is understanding. "Okay. Thank you for telling me." His shoulders loosen a fraction; the fox knocker approves with a non-existent wink—not literal—close enough. I keep going because I have to. "But don't tell me you're a coward and then ask me to make you brave by pretending I don't want you. That's not a job I'll take. I'll go slow," I add, softer. "I won't go 'small'."

His eyes lift to mine like a man checking a level. Something in them frays and ties again. "I don't want you small."

"Good." I set my palms on the table because I'm tempted to set them on him. "Then we need a language for days like this. Deliberate doesn't mean retreat. It means choose. If you need time, say 'time' and not 'distance'. If you need me near and not touching, say 'near.'" My throat gets stupidly tight. "Don't warm me and wander off. It's too cold here for that."

He takes it; I can see him take it, hands wrapping around the words like they're a tool he can use instead of a feeling he'll botch. "Near," he says, almost to himself, as if testing the weight. Then, to me: "Near."

We try it. It's terrible and perfect. We sit on the sofa with a quilt and a foot of air between our knees and talk like people learning the grammar of a new country. He tells me how the bank spoke to his da like a misbehaving dog and he swore he'd never ask anyone for anything he couldn't repay with work. I tell him about a man who called me too much, until I believed it and began carving out pieces to hand him until I was a neat bowl for his comfort. He stares at the fire like it insulted him. I laugh at the ceiling because otherwise I'll cry. The kettle hums second cups to keep our hands busy.

Wind shoulders the cottage and the latch mutters. Our pumpkins outside flicker and flare, holding steady. For one minute—two—we do the quiet bravery of staying in the room with a difficult truth and not trying to decorate it to make it go down easier. It is the worst kind of intimacy. It may be the best.

When the second hand on the mantel creaks to the half, he clears his throat. "Hay bales," he says, ridiculous and right. "Green. Hamish'll have started already. Come keep us from murdering each other with geometry."

My heart snaps towards him like a compass needle finding north. Not a retreat. A right turn. "Aye," I say, stealing the word and not apologising for it.

We layer ourselves in weather coats, scarf, my beanie pulled low. Outside, our pumpkins throw friendly circles on the wet stone. As we step past them, both flames lift at once with a soft whoomph, a small, synchronised reach. Somewhere up the brae, a fox barks once, neat as a nail tapped home.

The green is a mess of wet and intent. Hamish is shouting affectionate insults at two lads who insist physics is a suggestion. Mrs. Baxter is directing with a walking stick like a marshal of troops. Bales squat and grin, slick with rain. It's chaos. It's exactly what we need.

"Architect?" Hamish hollers at me. "Save us."

We scaffold the ceilidh floor with straw and stubbornness. I turn rows into lanes and lanes into a ring so dancers will have edges without feeling penned. Ethan carries ridiculous weights like he forgot gravity applies to him; he listens when I say 'there,' and carries them there, exactly. We don't touch. That's the pact for the hour. We do the next best thing: we look up and find each other across the green, two points on a line that wouldn't exist otherwise.

By the time the last bale sits proper, the sky has made a pale, reluctant truce with the town. We stand under the smith's awning, steam rising off our shoulders, breath visible and the kind you can taste if you're reckless. Ethan takes the paper cup of cider the smith shoves at him and blows across it like he's doing something more complicated. He's avoiding my mouth, which is fair; it's rude in public.

"Near?" he asks, voice low enough to be a private word in a busy place.

"Near," I say, and step so our arms brush. He doesn't flinch. He doesn't surge. He breathes like a man reprieved.

The geese choose that moment to sally forth from nowhere like drunk nobles demanding toll. One advances, neck stretched, eyes small and full of God. Ethan angles his body between me and the goose with the seriousness of a knight addressing a dragon. "Away," he tells it, in the special tone Scots use with creatures who don't understand English and still obey it. The goose considers, insults his lineage, retreats.

I laugh, too loud, all at once, the kind that unknots something. He tips his head; soft smile he doesn't show the town often. "There she is," he says, so quiet the hay must agree to keep the secret.

We carry that truce back to Rowan Lane. At my step he hesitates, puts a palm against the doorframe the way he did the night he fixed the hinge. "I'll go mind the shop," he says. Not an excuse. A thing that's true. "Then—if you want—come by after. I'll show you the curl in the oak you asked for."

He's offering me his private holy of holies to stand inside, hands in pockets, not touching the altar. Near. Choose. Not small.

"Yes," I say. The fox knocker approves with an expression beyond its metallurgy.

After he leaves, the cottage feels larger than its walls. The candle on the table wobbles, regains itself, burns steady. I stare at the laptop and the laptop stares back. A chime I've trained myself to dread pings: production error, US client, payment loop failing edge-cases. Somewhere a server is panicking, and customers are swearing. Excellent. A problem I can point a brain at.

I pull the quilt over my knees and go to war. Logs, stack traces, black coffee that tastes like an apology. My mind clicks into the clean place it loves—the land where cause and effect still shake hands like gentlemen. I find the greedy function. I teach it restraint. I write the tests it should have had and the ones it didn't know to ask for. When the code passes in a sweep, the sound it makes in my chest is not unlike relief after a held breath. People, it turns out, are harder than programs. But I can bring this house its small offerings of working things.

When I push the fix, the rain has behind-the-scenesed itself to a fine mist. I stand and my body does the list of complaints only a sofa can produce. The pumpkins still burn outside, steady as hearts.

I'm carrying the mugs to the sink when someone moves in the fogged glass of the window and my stomach does a fireworks-and-elevator drop combo. He's there. Not at the door—down the lane, under the lamplight, head tipped, watching my step like a man reading a ledger he hopes says, paid.

I could call. I don't. I open the door.

He turns, smile unforced, gratitude like a bruised fruit he's decided not to hide. "The curl's waiting," he says.

Behind him, the world puts on a show too neat to be anything but a bribe: the lamplight turning the smirr to fine gold rain, a paper moon slipping its knot and sailing down between us to land at our feet without tearing, the fox knocker on my door winking for the simple joy of it.

I step out and pull the door to. The pumpkins glow the colour of promises kept. He offers me his hand like a gentleman from a book and like a man from this town. I take it.

We walk towards the yard in a silence that feels like the 'aye' before a tune starts. We have not solved the whole of us; we have made a thing we can stand on when the wind gets up. It's not what I thought tension would be, back when I thought tension meant slammed doors and dramatic rain.

It's sharper and kinder than that. It has edges and a handle.

"Near," I say, just to hear the word keep us company.

"Aye," he says, and the yard gate opens like a door hung true.

Chapter 14 — Grainfire

Ethan's POV

The yard smells of wet oak and first frost, the kind of cold that makes breath honest. I unlatch the side gate and let it swing, palm riding the wood the way you do with something that's learned your hand. Samantha steps through at my shoulder, scarf tucked into my coat because she keeps stealing the things that keep me warm and I keep letting her.

"Show me the curl," she says, voice low like we're already inside the secret.

"Aye." I lead her past the stack of ash boards to the back wall where I keep the pieces that talk when light touches them. Rain's gone to a fine smirr; the yard lamp throws a pale coin on the tarpaulin. I take the corner and haud—lift—slow. The slab underneath gives itself up: pippy oak with a ribbon of curl through the heart, figure shimmering like a river's bed when the sun hits the riffle just right.

She inhales. "Oh." One soft syllable like a match taken to kindling.

I angle the lamp. The grain wakes, rolling under the surface—cat's paw, fiddleback, the curl you only get when a tree fought wind and won. "Some call it tiger," I say. "Some call it trouble. Looks like it's moving when you walk by."

"It is moving," she says, stepping, watching the light chase itself along the figure. "Like it's breathing. Like it remembers the storm." She lays her palm to the board—splayed fingers, care in the touch—and the wee hairs along my forearms stand up like the grain's telling me aye.

"Trees keep a ledger," I say before I can stop myself, because honesty has been nipping my heels all day. "Every year ring a story. Every knot a choice. You cut true and the truth shows. You cheat and it does, too."

She glances up, jaw settling like she's hearing more than I said. "Name it and it's twice true."

The wind shoulders the barn and the old tin roof complains. Somewhere beyond, the geese hold council and decide against us. I set the lamp down and her hand stays where it is, palm warm on oak, the light making a little glow under her skin as if the board's giving something back.

"Magic," she says, teasing and not.

"I told you I believed in things you can feel and not see." I set my palm over hers, the slab cool beneath, her skin heat above, the three layers speaking to each other in a language I know without names. The warmth of her climbs my wrist slow and certain. The yard tilts toward quiet. The world decides to behave.

She turns her hand under mine, fingers tracing my knuckles, then sliding to the bare skin at my wrist, pulse to pulse. She's not rushing me. She's setting the weight. "Near?" she asks, remembering our pact.

"Closer," I hear myself say, and it's a relief the size of a shed roof taken off without breaking.

We leave the lamp and the slab to talk to each other and drift around the far side of the barn where the yard throws a shadow that belongs to us. The grass there is damp and sweet; the air tastes of iron and apple peel. Beyond, the square clatters faintly—dishes, laughter, someone practising a tune that keeps failing and standing again. The corner is hidden from the lane, not scandalous, not exactly invited. A good place for the thing I mean to do.

She presses a shoulder to the timber; I put a palm beside her head, the rough plank biting the heel of my hand just enough to keep me awake. We're nose to nose. Her breath lifts the wool at my throat. The space between us is a hinge. We've sanded it. It swings easy now.

"Deliberate," she whispers, last benediction, first dare.

"Aye," I say, and close the inch we've been carrying since the bookshop door stuck, and the bunting leaf fell.

The kiss is heat without hurry, careful breaking into hunger, the soft clatter of a tool finding its slot and locking in. She tastes of apple and peat smoke and the kind of laughter that comes up from the bottom of a person and changes their face. Her hands find my jaw as if to steady us both; my own settle at the small of her back where she set them earlier, and everything that was tight in me all afternoon unknots with a sound I hope the barn boards keep to themselves.

She laughs—God, that laugh—when my beard rasps her lip, then makes a sound that isn't laughter at all when I angle and kiss deeper. The wind tugs at her beanie; I catch it, shove it into my pocket one-handed without breaking the kiss, and she smiles against my mouth like I've passed a test she didn't mean to set.

"Say when," I murmur, tasting the word on her lower lip.

"Don't," she says, hardly any sound in it. "Don't say when yet."

I don't. I say her name instead, and the syllables come out like a vow I'm not afraid of.

Heat climbs neat as a ladder: mouth, jaw, throat. I move to the place beneath her ear—the one I claimed under lanterns, the one that made a map of last night—and set my mouth there slow. Her knees soften; my hand finds her hip, tights slick under my palm, warmth a live thing behind the cloth. She tips her head, offering more, and I take no more than is given.

The yard lamp buzzes once and flares with a soft whoomph, then settles—not literal—close enough. On the far side, a tarp loosens its knot and spills a fall of sawdust into the air. The eddies spin and hang, catching light—a slow whirl of gold that looks very much like approval. Aye, well.

"Ethan," she breathes, then bites her smile because she knows what it does to me when my name leaves her mouth like that. I answer with my hands—one at the small of her back anchoring, one sliding up her spine under the edge of my coat she's wearing, my palm finding warm skin and stopping there like a man who knows the difference between rush and right.

She makes a wee desperate sound that goes straight down every line of me and sets the lot alight. I swallow it with a kiss and give her back something steadier—a rhythm, a place to stand inside want. She learns it quick—meets, retreats, finds; laughter breaking into sighs when I run my thumb along the seam of heat where her waist meets my palm; a soft curse in a friendly tongue when I shift my thigh and she fits.

From the lane, Hamish's voice sails like a seagull with opinions. We freeze, grinning against each other like bairns behind a dyke. His whistle drifts past the yard gate and keeps going. She presses her face to my neck and laughs silent, the shake of it doing blessedly ruinous things to my self-control.

"Bandit," I accuse, hands tightening.

"Carpenter," she returns, hands already in my hair. "Show me where to put this."

It's a daft line. It nearly finishes me.

"Here," I say, guiding her wrist to the back of my neck, that soft rope of muscle a man only remembers when someone good puts a hand there. "And here." I slide her other hand to my chest, where the rhythm's gone from tidy to a gallop, I'd fail for on any job site. "Feel me."

"I do." She says it like a discovery and a claim. "Mo… what was it you said?" Her mouth curves, drunk on language. "Mo chridhe?"

I close my eyes and survive that. "Aye," I say, rough. "Aye, that."

We kiss like we've accepted terms. The barn keeps us. The wind lifts and lays itself down. The lamp hums on. Somewhere, a fox barks once—a sharp nail tapped home.

Her hands wander, curious, sure. Mine do the same, guided by the map we drew, careful of boundaries we set and willing to find the edge again and press until it sings. I feel laughter spark in her even when she sighs; I feel sighs catch even when she laughs. It makes a holy mess of me and I let it, because this is the kind of breaking that mends into something stronger.

She chases my mouth with intent now, a coorie that isn't about keeping out the cold and everything to do with learning how to be hot without burning the place down. "Deliberate," she breathes into the seam where my lips part, and I show her deliberate like a craftsman shows a finished joint: no gap, no creak, no shame.

"Christ," I mutter when her teeth find my lower lip. She grins into the kiss, proud. "Dangerous lass."

"Only to cowards," she says, biting again, softer. Her fingers hook into my belt like a promise she's not cashing tonight and my body files a formal complaint with management.

I step back a breath to look—actually look—because she asked me this morning to choose with my eyes open. Her mouth is kiss-reddened; her hair's come wild where the beanie used to be; there's sawdust caught in her lashes from the spill. She's wearing my coat. She looks like winter made warmer and a home I'd build twice just to get it right.

"You're staring," she says, half-tease, half-question.

"I'm memorising," I admit, because this is a good country we've found and I mean to map it true. "If the roof blows off in a gale tomorrow, I'll still have this."

"It won't," she says, grave as a kirk bell. "You built it."

We stand there, breath turning white between us and folding away, and the wanting doesn't leave; it settles its weight honestly. I tip my forehead to hers. "Say when."

She tips mine back, the touch a benediction. "Not yet." Then—wicked, generous—"Soon."

"Aye." I can live in soon if the road is this.

She tugs me in again anyway and we steal one more kiss, quick and hot and grateful, before the yard remembers we're not the only folk in it. The smith's boy barrels past the gate, sees nothing, trips on a stray wedge, and swears in a whisper that would make Mrs. Baxter resign her commission. We laugh into each other's mouths like we've been caught nicking apples and mean to do it again.

"Come," I say, breath finding rhythm. "If I don't show you the ash that sings when you plane it, I'll lie awake thinking of you not knowing."

We round back to the stack. I take down a narrow board, set it on the trestle, and pull the small block plane from the bench. The blade's keen and the ash is in the mood to be beautiful. I set her hands first—thumb here, heel there—then wrap mine around to guide. The first pass lifts a pale curl that leaps like a fiddle string struck clean. It lands on her wrist, warm and weightless. Her face lifts, victorious, clean joy like a lantern.

"It sings," she says, soft and fierce. "You weren't being poetic. It actually sings."

"I'm never poetic," I lie, because a man has to keep some reputation.

We take another pass together. Shavings puddle at our elbows like snow that never thought to be cold. Her body moves with mine—weight forward, pull back, reset—finding the job's rhythm the way she's been finding mine. When her breath syncs to it, I'm a goner.

"Lesson ends or we're doing this in a sermon," I mutter, because restraint is a tool like any other.

"Later," she says, bright and unrepentant. "We'll attend church properly."

"Blasphemer." I put the plane down before I start teaching her how to hold it by muscle memory and wake up on the wrong side of deliberate. "Walk you back?"

"Please." She slides her hands into my coat pockets because she is a menace, and the pockets are mine and now they're hers.

We lock the barn, and the yard falls behind like a secret we'll keep better by sharing it. On Rowan Lane the pumpkins practise patience, steady as hearts, throwing circles that meet and become one between our boots—twin light making one pool. The fox knocker girds himself to mischief—not literal—close enough. I don't kiss her at the door because we're both laughing too hard for it to land how it should— Hamish shouts something about hay geometry from the corner; a cat takes violent exception to a leaf. But I do put my hand at the small of her back, with her permission still warming it, and feel her lean just enough that the bones of my hand will remember.

"Tomorrow," she says, hand on the fox like a pact. "Baking with the girls. You?"

"Fence for Mrs. Mackie," I say. "If it doesn't hold, I'll never live it down."

"Balance," she says, and the word feels like a jam jar put up after harvest. "Then dinner? I'll bring something that doesn't require talent."

"Bring yourself." I reach, touch her jaw with two fingers, a light tap where my beard made a mark. "I'll sort the rest."

She kisses my fingertips—deliberate devil—and my knees go interesting for a second. "Night, carpenter."

"Night, sunshine."

She slips inside. The blue door settles. The fox winks because he's a liar and we both like him that way—not literal—close enough. I stand in the lane feeling like a roof I hung true: weight above, house below, one small honest ember burning behind my ribs because we lit it and we're minded to keep it.

Behind the barn, the sawdust I spilled eddies once in a breathless corner and drops like a blessing. —not literal— close enough.

Chapter 15 — Bread & Fences

Samantha's POV

Glenkeld wakes gentle, like a quilt being shaken out over the town. The sky is a pale plate; the air's got that smirr that doesn't quite count as rain but blesses everything anyway. My pumpkins glow faintly under the blue door's eaves, smug as cats. Inside, the kettle hums, the fox knocker winks—outrageous—not literal—close enough, and somewhere a fiddle string tests the morning with a hopeful note and decides to keep going.

"Balance," I tell the cottage, because houses deserve a headline for the day. "Baking and fences. Dough and nails. You and me."

The phone buzzes where it's nested in my scarf. *Fence first,* Ethan's text reads. *Mackie's ewe tested the laws of physics at dawn. Back by five. Dinner?* A beat later: *Near.*

Near, I type back. *And dinner. I'll bake something that won't cause an insurrection.* I add a fox emoji. The fox knocker preens—not literal—close enough.

By ten, Morag's back room has turned into a sugar-dusted battleground. A long table, flour like snowdrift, a chorus of women—Katie with a sprig of rosemary in her hair; Mrs. Baxter, marshal of bakes and morals; two mums with weans underfoot, faces already smeared with jam. The window is fogged with breath and oven heat. We are making cinnamon knots for the ceilidh and pretending this requires two battalions and a general.

"Ye sift," Morag orders, pressing a sieve into my hands like a weapon. "And haud your elbow steady. Flour's like gossip—must be spread fine or it clumps."

"I'll never look at sifting the same way," I say, obedient, showering the bowl with the soft drift of white.

"It's the only sermon I preach," she says, eyes twinkling. "That and: add more butter. Aye, Katie?"

"Always butter," Katie confirms, bashfully tucking hair behind her ear, and then flushes when Hamish's laughter sails past outside like a gull with a crush.

We get to work. Dough is a living thing in a small town—breathing under the towel, risings like held breath released. I warm milk to not-quite-hot and watch the yeast wake, a fizz of life. Morag's hands are brisk, capable, not gentle exactly but respectful, the way you handle a person you like who knows their own mind. Mrs. Baxter approves or humphs as required. The mums roll little snakes for the kids to twist into knots; the children take this as a solemn vocation and then eat their creations raw with glee.

"Tell us," Katie says, careful casual, rolling out a sheet the size of a pillowcase. "Is the carpenter a decent sort indoors as he is out? Does he put his tools away? Does he—"

"Katie," Mrs. Baxter warns, but her mouth quirks. "Let the lass speak if she likes."

I dust my hands, aware of four pairs of eyes pretending not to stare. "He mends what he touches," I say, feeling heat climb my neck and not disliking it. "He listens before he lifts a tool. He doesn't take what isn't given. And he believes in fires fed slow."

Morag makes a sound that might be a benediction and might be glee. "Aye," she says, satisfied. "That's my boy."

Katie grins into her dough. "And ye do look a bit smitten, hen."

"I'm smitten," I admit, rolling sugar and cinnamon into the sheet, feeling the fragrant sand under my palms. "Deliberately."

We twist ropes, knot them, tuck the ends under like secrets. Butter melts and carries cinnamon into the air; the room goes quiet in that way kitchens do when everybody falls into rhythm. Outside, the smirr turns to nothing. The sky brightens like a promise paid.

Somewhere on the far edge of town, Ethan shoulders a fence post into the earth. I can feel it the way you feel weather—under the skin. The thought rolls through me and settles everything where it belongs.

"Proofed," Mrs. Baxter declares, tapping the dough. "Into the heat. Watch your knuckles or you'll learn new words."

We slide trays into the oven and the whole room breathes, ah, in unison as if we've just been told a good story with a happy ending. Tea appears. Doughnuts materialise. Someone puts a record on—old, crackling, a reel that makes the toddlers hop like corn over flame. I sit on the sill, cup warming my hands, and let myself be held by this small domestic machine: the whisking, the laughter, the shouts up

Autumn in Glenkeld: Pumpkins & Firelight

the close, Morag shooing Hamish when he tries to sneak a raw knot and fails.

"Balance," Mrs. Baxter says, following my gaze to the window where the square unspools its day. "You can love a lad and still bake your own bread. You can set a fence and still dance a reel. Set both right and the wind can do as it pleases."

I tuck that somewhere safe. "Aye," I say, and the word sits sweet on my tongue, a loaner turned resident.

The knots come out brown and glossy, faces on a choir, edges sticky with sugar. We brush them with heather honey and the scent rises like a hymn. We box them with tissue and gossip—this tray for the kirk, this for the pie raffle, this to be "lost" on Ethan's bench later. Katie slips two into a paper bag and pushes it at me. "Emergency rations," she says, eyes bright. "For fence inspectors."

I don't say out loud that I'm learning the small weight of belonging, how it sits differently from obligation. I just take the bag and tuck it into my scarf like a relic.

— — —

Out by the Mackie place, the world is a different hymn: wet earth, a dog with ideas, the sharp clack of hammer on staple, Ethan's low voice talking to timber. I find him by following both the noise and the feeling under my breastbone that points the way to him like a compass trying to be subtle.

He's stripped down to a shirt despite the chill, sleeves rolled, forearms sawdust-kissed. A fence post leans against his shoulder as he measures the line with his eye. Mr. Mackie talks with his hands; Mrs. Mackie has made a thermos of soup big enough to drown a man. The dog—Tansy—tries to steal Ethan's glove and does not get away with it.

He sees me and the careful part of his face eases, the way a door lifts a hair when it's hung true and stops catching. "Inspector," he says, half-smile. "We're near."

"Closer," I say, because words are our work. I hold up the bag. "Bribe."

It's greedy, how fast his eyes go soft. "You're a witch," he says, and takes a knot, and when he bites the icing strings in a way that is not decent, I forget why people invented other foods.

We arrange ourselves into usefulness. I hold a post while he checks the level—my fingers under his, warm against wood, a neat little shock like the grain decided to approve us. Tansy supervises with her whole tail. When a cloud tries to spit, it changes its mind; the sky has been generous all day and means to see the thing through.

"Here," he says, passing me the hammer, palm to palm. "You're plenty strong. Take the middle staples. I'll finish the low."

We work until my shoulders know about it. He drops down to the damp to set the bottom line, kneeling in mud without complaint, and when he looks up, there's dirt on his jaw and a crack of sun on his cheekbone and the kind of pride in his eyes that makes everything else I thought was exciting feel like a false start.

"Fence'll hold," he says, standing, stretching. "Even with an ewe who dreams of Paris."

"I do like a girl with plans," I say, and he laughs, warm and surprised, that sound I keep wanting to bottle.

Mr. Mackie insists on feeding us soup we can stand a spoon in. We eat leaning against the good fence, our knees touching like an unspoken vow. Mrs. Mackie approves of the knots like a woman seeing her future in pastry. Tansy collapses across Ethan's boots because she knows where solidity lives.

When we say we'll be at the ceilidh tomorrow—of course we will—Mrs. Mackie claps like a bell. "Bring your girl," she tells Ethan, without looking at me, because older women understand the power of naming. "We'll keep a spot near the band. Best acoustics for falling in love."

"Ma'am," Ethan says, bashful and taller somehow. "Aye."

— — —

By late afternoon, Glenkeld is polished. The smirr has gone; the square wears a thin gold of sunshine that feels like a favour granted. I walk home with my basket smelling like butter and sugar and blether. Ethan peels off to wash up and "put my face right," which is ludicrous because his face is unfair without trying. We agree on near, on six, on dinner at mine with ingredients that don't require talent—bread, cheese, apples, soup I pretend to have made and actually did because Morag has turned me into a witch of the practical kind.

The blue door greets me with the small pride of a house that's been expecting company. I set a pot to warm, slice a loaf, cut apples into moons. The fox knocker inserts himself into the reflected glass and practices smirking. I light the pumpkins; both wicks catch with a soft whoomph—not literal—close enough. Our two faces throw friendly circles that overlap on the step and become one long pill of gold—twin light making one pool.

When the knock comes, it's gentle. The door opens on Ethan in a clean flannel, hair damp from a comb, a bouquet that is not flowers but late rosemary and bay from Katie's spare, wrapped in brown paper with twine. He looks big in my small room in the way a tree makes a clearing feel intended, not crowded.

"Hi," he says, and it's astonishing how 'hi' can be a full-body experience.

"Hi," I answer, and step straight into him because the day has been full of good work and I want the reward that belongs to it.

The kiss is warm bread and relief, steady, unshowy, an old tune made new by two voices finding the same key. His hand finds the small of my back like it has learned that route and intends to wear it into a path. I taste cinnamon and fence post and gratitude. He tastes like my name said in a quiet room.

"Dinner," I say against his mouth, because there is soup and because I am a woman of my word. "Then maybe we…not yet but—"

Autumn in Glenkeld: Pumpkins & Firelight

"Soon," he says, finishing me with that soft certainty I'm starting to trust. "Deliberate."

We eat like people who have learned the magic of ordinary: soup that tastes like comfort, bread that argues with butter and loses, apples that explode light on the tongue. He tells me Tansy stole his glove again; I tell him Mrs. Baxter can proof dough by glare alone. We laugh in the same places. It's not showy. It feels like a house settling the last tiny millimetre onto its foundation with a sound only the two of us hear.

After, I put the kettle on and he—without making a speech of it—rises to wash the bowls, sleeves shoved up, forearms slick, water turning his soap bubbles into galaxies. Domesticity slays me in a way no grand gesture ever has. I lean in the doorway and watch a man make my kitchen look as if it was drawn around him.

The fox knocker winks. The candle on the table flares with a soft whoomph as if taking notes. The pumpkins on the step hold steady even when a wind fingers the lane. Balance, I think again, and the word fits better than it did this morning.

"Come here," he says, when the last bowl is set to dry, and I do, and we stand with tea cooling between our hands, foreheads touching, the room humming like it gets to keep us.

"Tell me something true," I ask, because I'm greedy.

He considers, eyes open, not hiding in the easy. "I looked at a slab today and thought, I want to make a table that keeps her elbows and her stories." He clears his throat, faintly abashed. "That's a daft thing to say aloud."

"It's not," I say, and the yes that rises in me makes my eyes sting in a good, dangerous way. "Make the table. I'll fill it."

His palm cups my jaw, thumb at the soft point where my pulse lives. "Aye."

We don't tip into heat tonight in the way the storm asked us to. We could. God, we could. The want is a warm animal in the corner, patient, well-fed. But the day has been about hands and work and the small seams you sew so the big ones hold. We make out like teenagers in my kitchen—yes, thoroughly. "Say when," he murmurs against my mouth. "Not yet," I whisper, smiling. "Soon." We stop with breathless grins and noses bumped and the fox looking like he's writing scandal, and it feels like winning.

When he leaves—late, lantern in hand, the lane kind—he pauses at the threshold and sets his palm to the doorframe the way he always does, a communion I don't pretend to understand and don't need to.

"Tomorrow," he says. "Ceilidh. Dance with me."

"I'll fall over your boots," I warn, delighted to have something so ordinary to warn him of.

"I'll mind your steps," he says, and there's a heat under it that promises other kinds of minding. "Near?"

"Near," I say, and kiss the corner of his mouth where last night's beard left its memory, and the candle on the table flares with a soft whoomph as if taking notes—not literal—close enough.

After he's gone, I blow out the pumpkins and the room clenches into the sweet dark that belongs to places that have held good conversation. I wash the last spoon, stroke the fox's ridiculous head, and set my hands flat on the table to feel the grain and think about a future slab of oak with curl that will learn our elbows.

Balance. Dough and nails. Bread and fences. A woman who knows what she wants and a man who's learning how to carry the weight of it without dropping his own name.

Outside, a fox barks once, neat as a nail tapped home. Inside, I answer with a small, satisfied, aye, and the house remembers the word.

Chapter 16 — Wild Weather, Kept Promises
Ethan's POV

The afternoon behaves itself right up until it doesn't.

I'm closing the shop—bench oiled, planes sheathed, stove banked—when the wind turns on its heel and comes down off Ben Carna with opinions. First a smirr like a warning, then the kind of rain that lines up and marches. The lane runs silver between the cobbles; the paper moons on Morag's awning knock together like teeth.

I text *ceilidh still on tomorrow—near?* and get back *near, aye* with a fox emoji I pretend not to like as much as I do. I mean to put on a stew, mind the fire.

Instead, the bell over the door rings and brings the storm in wearing my scarf and a grin.

Samantha's hair is wet at the ends, eyes bright with mischief and weather. "So," she says, bracing the door shut with her back while the wind tests it, "are you collecting stray Americans again, or shall I try to swim to Rowan Lane?"

"Get in," I say, and the word lands like an act: let this be the place. I slide the bolt, lift the kettle, and loosen my shoulders because good things are easier when a man remembers to.

"It turned fast," she says, peeling off my scarf and handing it to me like a fond theft. "I was halfway and thought, well, the geese will be wearing life jackets."

"They'll be appointing themselves harbourmaster," I say, and that gets her laughing, and the shop looks warmer for it.

The rain goes from steady to a drumroll on the tin roof. The gutter outside takes offence and starts to overflow at the elbow. I make the small calculation I've made twice now—bridge to the burn, floorboards at her place, the fact that storms like to play king of the hill on that stretch of lane—and come up with the same answer. "We'll wait it."

She glances towards the back door that isn't just a door. The storm rattles the panes like a bored God. "Aye," she says, soft, choosing with me. "We'll wait it."

The kettle makes its pre-boil mutter. I reach for the hook, take down the towel, and catch her hands because they're cold and because I can. I rub warmth into each finger, thumb circling the knuckle, the old ritual that works on weather and nerves both. The look she gives me says 'thank you' and something slower that lands under the ribs and sits there purring.

"Deliberate," she says, a smile tucked in it.

"Aye."

We cross through.

The cabin knows her shape now; it rearranges itself the way a good room will for a returning person. The hearth is half-hearted; I set tinder, kindling, a wee peat brick, and the fire remembers its job with a soft whoomph. Light moves across the ceiling like a blessing. The fox on the mantel watches with the insolence of a creature that expects entertainment.

"Hi, you," she tells it, and the carved brute looks smug—not literal—close enough. Aye, well.

Her coat is beaded with rain. I slide it from her shoulders, hang it on the peg, feel heat leap along my palm where wool gives way to her. She's in a soft jumper, damp at the cuffs; my shirt from last night is folded neatly on the back of the chair because I am a man who plans to tempt fate.

"It'll pass," I say, because storms like flattery. The roof answers with a soft whoomph that rattles the spoon jar. We both laugh and stop closer than we started. The sound gets caught somewhere between us and turns into something else.

"What do you need?" she asks. Not coy. Not loaded. Just a woman in a warm room with clean wants.

"Truth," I say, because the thing about good answers is you don't have to invent new ones for new weather. "To keep you warm. To be careful and not coward. To…" I clear my throat because the last bit is the one that makes a man shy. "To make this a night we can stand inside when wind gets up later."

Her eyes soften. "Aye," she says, and then, wrecking me with kindness, "Near. Closer."

We don't rush the door. We lock it. We check the hinges. Then we step through.

Tea first, because nerves have better manners with cups in their hands. We stand at the hearth and drink until the fog on the window is not just weather. Our mugs sit side by side, twin ribbons of steam making one curl of warmth. The storm shoulders the eaves; the fire answers with cheek. We talk about nothing—Hamish's geometry crimes, Mrs. Baxter's dough glare, Katie's rosemary tucked behind her ear. Words settle my bones. Silence finishes the work.

"Deliberate," she murmurs, setting her mug down. Steam wraps her cheek; the fire coins her hair.

"Aye," I echo, and my hands find the shape of her waist like they've been pocketing that curve all day.

The first kiss does not knock furniture over. It doesn't need to. It's an opening move we've both practised in smaller rooms: the soft meet, the check for yes, the pressure that says, 'I'm here as long as you are'. Her hands slide to my jaw, thumb finding the place that loosens my lungs; my mouth finds the place at her lip that makes her inhale break into a laugh and then back into a kiss.

Heat climbs. Not a ladder, this time, but a slow, sure tide. I crowd her into the warm angle where hearth meets bookcase and the cabin approves with a lift of the flame. She hauls me closer by my shirt like she's claiming salvage, and the sound I make will not impress Mrs. Baxter but would earn me points in other circles.

"Say when," I manage, because consent sounds better spoken out loud, even if we've been speaking it with every inch.

"Not yet," she says, and then bites my lower lip once like punctuation and steals my good sense with it. "Soon. Now."

We don't undress like actors in a bad play. We unfasten slowly, untying weather, shifting cloth with care for buttons and for people. Her jumper rises; my hands find heat; the sound she makes lands where a man keeps religion. My Henley goes, and her palm learns the map it started last night, the line of scar at my rib, the place where breath sits when I name her. The fox pretends to look away. He does not.

We end up on the rug because rugs are what warmth invented for itself. The storm makes a racket like applause; we ignore it in favour of smaller truths. I lay her back; she pulls me with her; the room narrows to the honey heat of skin and the rhythm we've learned on lamp-lighted nights and felt under street lamps but not like this, not with the weather making a drum of our roof and the fire at our knees. She tastes of tea and rain and the word 'mine' said without hurry.

"Ethan," she breathes into the corner of my mouth, and I would hang doors for a thousand winters to hear that again.

"Aye," I answer, and prove it.

What happens next is the opposite of clever and the opposite of careless. We take our time until time gives up objecting. She asks with hands; I answer with mouth; I ask with breath; she answers with the lift of her body and a laugh that breaks and returns. When I go too fast she lays a palm to my jaw—here, hold—and when she goes quiet to feel, I make quiet a place worth staying. We learn each other like craft: repetition without boredom, attention without suspicion, a reverence for how good materials behave when you work with and not against.

At some point a gust rattles the latch. The lights remember they exist and forget again. The hearth throws a soft whoomph that wobbles the candle flame into a perfect wee heart—not literal—close enough. I am not a man for omens. I am a man for rooms, and this one is telling me we're doing fine.

"Mo chridhe," I say, not careful now, and the word lands where pulse lives under her skin. She pulls me down by the back of my neck and answers with my name like a bell rung soft and true.

We cross the point that separated last night's almost from tonight's all the way without finding it with our feet. The want that's been a warm animal in the corner pads over and lays its head between our ribs. We don't feed it the whole woodpile; we give it the good logs and watch it take, steady and bright. The line breaks into surrender at the same time for both of us—with a gasp and a laugh and something that feels like weather changing—and I find myself grateful in a way that makes my bones feel like they've been scrubbed.

After, I lie there and listen to the cabin settle its creaks around our new temperature. The storm moves to the far hill to try its luck there. Her breath rides my collarbone like a boat tied up safe. The fox looks insufferable. The candle burns straight and tall as a boy who's decided to behave.

"Still here?" she asks against my throat, husky with use.

"Aye." I turn my head and kiss her hair, damp with different weather. "Long as you'll have me."

"That long," she says, audacious and soft.

We drift but don't sleep. The lull between storms belongs to talk. She tells me about writing code that catches edge-cases the way a good fence catches ewes with Paris on their mind. I tell her about the slab of oak I've been saving for no reason I could name yesterday and can name today. We plan the table. We plan nothing else except more of this on terms we can keep.

When the rain finds its second wind and drums again, the fire answers like a beast turning over, pleased. Heat comes back to our hands; it goes to our mouths; the wanting wakes like it only dozed. We fall into each other with less care and no less kindness. Slow turns quick and then slows again at the right edges. Spice rolls—laughter and gasps, a soft curse, a whispered, aye, and a fiercer one. I keep my palm at the small of her back because that's where it belongs now; she keeps her hand in my hair because I told her it steadies me and she filed it under useful.

"Christ," I say when she finds me exactly wrong and exactly right with a thumb and a wicked smile.

"Language," she scolds, breathless, then: "No, keep it. Say more."

So, I do, and she learns I can be a poet after all when the audience is right.

We make a mess of the rug and the tidy lines we pretend to keep, and when we're done being clever about restraint we let it go until the room fogs and the window writes its name and the candle has to remind us it's still there. It is not the first time. It won't be the last. It feels like the first and last at once, which is how you know you did it honestly.

Autumn in Glenkeld: Pumpkins & Firelight

Later—tea again, because bodies are small animals who like ritual—we sit with the quilt over our knees like pensioners who've committed a scandal. She leans into my shoulder; I rest my chin in her hair; the world shrinks down to this wicket of light and two mugs.

"I want to dance with you tomorrow and not look at my feet," she says, drowsy and formidable.

"I'll mind your steps," I tell her. "And if we fall, we'll do it in time."

She laughs, soft. "Tell me something true."

I look at the framed doorway to the shop, at the bench beyond, at the racks of tools sleeping like well-fed dogs. "I wake up alone most mornings and don't notice," I say. "I'll notice now."

She goes quiet in that way that means 'I heard you and I'll carry it carefully.' "Then we'll have a plan," she says. "Some mornings mine. Some yours. Some we'll make up as we go."

"Aye." I swallow. "Stay."

"Deliberate," she says. "Aye."

We bank the fire but not all the way. We leave the candle and the fox to their gossip. In the nook, the bed earns its keep. We find sleep and lose it and find it again like sheep who remember the gate and then forget. When the storm moves off for good, the roof exhales. So, do I.

Before I go under, I feel her fingers write something on my forearm in the dark—nonsense letters, a habit of bodies that trust the room to keep secrets. I answer with my palm open on her hip: here, here, here.

"Mo chridhe," I say one more time to the ceiling and the beam, to see if the word still fits. It does.

Outside, a fox barks once—quick as a nail tapped home—and the ember in the grate rounds itself again into that daft wee heart, bright as a vow you mean to keep.

Chapter 17 — Honeyed Midnight
Samantha's POV

Night comes down soft as wool.

The storm has wandered off to bother another glen, leaving behind a sky rinsed black and cold enough to make the windowpanes haud their breath. Ethan's hearth glows in a low, satisfied way—the kind of fire that's done the hard work and is ready to sit with you. The room smells of peat and clean skin and a ghost of cinnamon from the knot I pressed into his palm hours ago. The fox on the mantel pretends not to watch and absolutely watches.

We should be sleeping.

Instead, we're a tangle on the rug, quilt half-dragged down to the floor because beds are too far away and the world's gone small in the best way—two mugs cooling on the table; twin ribbons of steam making one curl of warmth, our pumpkins outside holding their warm coins on the step as if guarding the door. My body's loose with the good kind of ache; my heart is crisp around the edges, like a leaf that turned gold overnight.

Ethan's hand is a weight at the small of my back, the place he seems to steady on instinct now. My name still lives in the room from earlier—said reverent, said wrecked, said like a promise—and when I shift closer his breath stumbles, soft and honest.

"We should sleep," I whisper, absolutely not meaning it.

"We should," he agrees in the tone of a man who plans to sin by omission. "Tomorrow's the ceilidh. Hamish will mock our footwork for months."

"Let him," I say, and push my nose into that particular warm place under his jaw where his pulse lives. His fingers flex on my spine like a "hello, then," and the answering hello in me is a bright thing I don't bother hiding.

"Tell me what you want," he murmurs, burr heavier in the late hour, restraint turned velvet.

The old me would have turned this moment into a test: make him guess, make him prove it. The woman on this rug—the one who's been fed bread and honey and aye—doesn't need to play at scarcity. I lift my head, meet the grey of his eyes made dark by fire, and say it.

"More," I breathe, shameless and pleased. "Closer. Slow until it's not. And—" the word feels like stepping onto a new stone in a stream and finding it solid "—I want to tell you yes without worrying I'll disappear."

He exhales through his nose like a laugh that's decided to be a prayer. "Aye. I can work with that."

He doesn't reach. He asks. A question asked with mouth and hand and the whole of his careful body. He rolls to face me, bracing on an elbow, and puts his palm at my jaw like a craftsman setting a piece before the first pass—checking the grain, respecting the line. "Our words?" he says.

"Our words," I echo. "Near, closer. Say when. Not yet, soon." I add, because I want the safety net strung tight, "Stop means stop."

"Aye." He kisses the agreement into the corner of my mouth. "Stop means stop."

When he kisses me properly, the room leans in. There's a patience to it that isn't for show; it's how he moves through the world—attention first, pressure second, rhythm found not forced. He maps me again like it's a pleasure, not a duty: my cheek, my jaw, the soft place at my neck he seems to have claimed under lanterns and storm, the stretch of collarbone that makes my breath misbehave. I find him back with hands and mouth—relearn the tendon at the back of his neck that steadies when I hold it, the scar at his rib that says he's lived, the way his lower lip yields and then answers.

"Say when," he prompts, voice gone to warm gravel, mouth at my ear.

"Not yet," I say, and the fox on the mantel—inexcusable creature—winks—not literal—close enough—like a midwife.

We unfasten deliberately, the way we did earlier, but with a new fluency, the shorthand you earn after you've read the long version aloud. Cloth shifts, skin answers, the fire puts a small, pleased soft whoomph into the air and settles smugly into itself. He presses a kiss to the inside of my wrist like an old-world vow; I hook my ankle behind his knee and tug him closer because I am not an old-world anything.

"I like you bossy," he says, wrecked and admiring.

"I like you ruinable," I return, and the laugh that shakes his chest is a full-body yes.

Heat has ways with us. It climbs, retreats, returns, like a reel that keeps finding the step it loves. Outside, the smirr has gone; the lane is crisp with frost. Inside, we're summer tucked in tartan. He knows how to place his hands—wide and sure, not a whisper of hurry. I know how to ask now—here, there, too much, just right—because he taught me that wanting is not a weapon and yes is a sentence you can rest in.

"Mo chridhe," he says again, not careful with the Gaelic, and the way my name comes after it is a string pulled through velvet. Something in me that's always kept a little back walks itself to the centre of the room and sits down.

"Again," I ask, greedy. "And use your hands."

He does, and I stop thinking in nouns for a while.

We are not quiet. We're not loud in a way that would have Mrs. Baxter banging a broom on the wall either. We're…honest. Laughter breaks the tension and makes a new, better kind. A sigh turns into a gasp, into a curse in two dialects, into a kiss with teeth. When I go still to listen to my body, he makes stillness feel like a thing you do together. When he loses the thread, I put my palm to his jaw and say "here" and his whole face does something I would knock on wood for if my hands weren't busy.

He doesn't take shortcuts. When he finds a sweetness, he lingers. When I gasp, he holds, not as a test, but because he's a man who minds the fire: feed, wait, watch, feed. The room approves. I can feel it. The candle on the table lifts its flame into a perfect wee heart and the ember in the grate brightens when he says my name like the timber itself is listening.

At some point, he stops my rush with a thumb at my hip, and the control in it makes me swear in gratitude. "Watch," he says, rough, eyes never leaving mine. "Let it take."

It does.

It takes in a tide, then a ripple, then a sudden, shameless lift that leaves me laughing, head tipped back, the ceiling a sky I invented just now. Ethan follows a heartbeat after with a sound that I'd like to bottle and label 'for emergencies.' He drops his forehead to mine, breath ragged, smile slant and soft—there you are and there I am in the same curve.

We rest messy and alive in a heap that would make a kirk lady cross herself and then bless us anyway. The fire purrs. Outside, somewhere distant, a fox barks once, neat as a nail tapped home.

After is my favourite part. Maybe it always will be. We drift in a warm harbour, naming small things because the big thing is obvious.

"I like your hands," I say, extremely profound.

"I like your mouth," he replies, choosing violence. Then, gentler: "I like the way you ask."

"Practice," I say.

He kisses my temple. "Keep practicing. I'll meet you."

We drink the last lukewarm inches of tea because bodies are small animals who like ritual. He pulls the quilt up; I coorie my toes under his calf. The ceiling makes those sweet old-house ticks that mean the day did not break anything essential.

"Tell me something true," I ask, because the question fits this hour the way peat fits flame.

He thinks with his eyes open the way he does when a joint needs setting true. "I used to think peace meant emptiness," he says slowly. "No noise, no want, no weather. Tonight, I learned peace can be…full. Warm. Heavy in the hands and easy in the heart." He swallows. "You did that."

I pretend not to cry by aiming my face at his shoulder. "Then do something for me," I say into flannel.

"Name it."

"Don't put yourself on a leash to keep me safe," I say. "Use your hands. Set the pace. I'll tell you if you go wrong. I'll tell you if you go right. But don't disappear yourself to prove you're careful."

The heat that moves through him is not lust exactly. It's relief. "Aye," he says, and I can feel the word land in his bones. "I can do that."

"Good." I tilt up, kiss the cut of his jaw. "Also—tomorrow, at the ceilidh, when I trip over your boots—"

"I'll mind your steps," he says, automatic, and then grins. "And make it look like you meant it."

We don't intend to tip back into heat. We absolutely do. This time it's slower, deeper—the kind of wanting that hums instead of crackles. We talk while we find it. We don't stop to apologise for how much we want. If there are boundaries left, we find their shape with careful fingers and write our names on them with laughter. When I ask for something, I have never said out loud and he gives it back to me exactly as asked, I feel a piece of myself I thought was ornamental click into usefulness.

"Say when," he murmurs at the last, voice blown to velvet.

"S—soon," I manage, and we balance there together like dancers who've finally stopped looking at their feet.

When sleep does come, it's the clean kind. We fold ourselves into the nook at last, quilt pulled up, fire dropped to embers. He tucks me under his chin and I draw a nonsense pattern on his forearm with a fingertip—loops and ladders, new lines written on old grain. He answers with the steady weight of his hand at my hip, the permission of it, the promise.

Outside, frost etches its quiet lace on the lane. "Tomorrow we dance," I say to the dark.

"Aye," he says into my hair. "And tonight we keep warm."

"Mo chridhe," I try, mangling the vowel on purpose so he'll correct me.

"Mo chridhe," he repeats, right and kind, and the ember in the grate rounds itself—just for a heartbeat—into a small, sure heart before relaxing back into glow —not literal—close enough.

Chapter 18 — Thunder in the Grain
Ethan's POV

Sometime after midnight the wind changes its mind.

It comes down off Ben Carna in a hurry, rattling the tin with a drummer's wrists and shouldering the eaves like an old friend who forgot how to knock. The cabin answers in its own language—rafters settling, the hearth giving a soft whoomph as a peat brick catches anew, the fox on the mantel making that insolent shadow across the beam as if he meant to enjoy the show.

Samantha stirs under my chin and makes the smallest sound—a pleased hum shaped like my name—and my body forgets what rest is for.

We should sleep. We said we would. Tomorrow there's the ceilidh and the town will want our feet. But her hair is warm against my mouth, and the night is brass and velvet at once, and I am a man whose hands have learned a map he can't stop tracing.

"Still warm?" I whisper into the crown of her head.

"Aye," she says, Scottish and smug, and presses back into me like the answer has weight.

The room has that late-hour honesty: every small thing louder, every breath a promise you either mean or don't. The pumpkins on the step glow low and stubborn—their circles overlapping into one small pool of gold—twin light making one pool. Rain tries the panes and then gives up; the wind takes over and makes a song of the gutter. Somewhere out past the yard, a fox barks once.

"Deliberate?" I ask, because our word is a hinge and I like swinging it true.

She turns in my arms, cheek sliding along my chest, and tips her face up. "Deliberate," she echoes, and then—wrecking me for good—adds, "Closer."

I'm undone before I move.

We take it slow, not because virtue insists, but because pleasure does. I kiss her like I'm testing a joint—pressure, release, the small turn that finds the tight fit. She answers with those honest hands, one at my jaw, one at the back of my neck where a man's certainty lives; every time her fingers settle there, the rest of me follows orders.

"Say when," I murmur, mouth at the corner of hers.

"Not yet," she says, and then makes a sound that takes the top board off my good sense when my palm finds the warm line of her waist under the quilt. The fox's shadow widens on the wall. The candle on the table—brazen thing—lifts to a straighter flame with a soft whoomph—not literal—close enough.

We unfasten slowly, untying the night like string from a parcel. Her shoulder finds air; I kiss it with the reverence you save for things that make you honest. My shirt leaves, delayed only by her insistence on taking it off herself, a small act of mischief that sends heat along my spine like a struck string. We don't knock furniture; we make gravity come to us.

"Mo chridhe," I tell the place under her ear, because Gaelic is stronger than I am right now.

She shivers, not with cold. "Again," she asks, greedy and righteous, and I give it to her until the word feels built into the beam.

Wind shoves the roof; the hearth answers like an animal turning over. The storm is the chorus; we're the tune. I find her mouth again, slower this time, and the kiss deepens from want to knowing, from knowing to a shared ruin that makes me laugh into it, stupid with joy. She laughs back and that's worse, better; then the sound breaks like thin ice under a boot when I drag my teeth, careful, along the line of her jaw. She gets even with a thumb at my lower lip that makes my hips forget what they're supposed to be doing.

"Bossy," I tell her, adoring it.

"Ruinable," she reminds me, wicked. "Prove it."

Aye, then.

We go from kiss to heat like a river finds the sea—no seam, only inevitability. I take my time with her, the way I do with wood that wants to be beautiful: let the grain tell me where to go, follow the figure, mind the knots that make the whole. When she gasps, I hold; when she laughs I press; when she goes still to feel I make quiet a country we can both live in. She tells me here, there, more, and the words land where hands should be.

Outside, the wind leans hard and sets the gutter to clapping. Inside, we make our own weather. The quilt goes crooked; we don't fix it. The rug is a conspiracy and we're part of it. A curl of hair sticks to her cheek; I smooth it back and her mouth finds my palm in thanks, then uses teeth, and I say a theological word my da would have washed my mouth for. She tells me to say it again. I do.

"Stop means stop," I remind, for both of us, not because we need it in this second but because we've promised to keep it close.

"Mhm," she says, and kisses the promise into my throat so I'll remember later, and then says the opposite and equally holy thing—"Don't stop,"—in a tone that takes my knees out from under me.

We roll—slow, careful—like folk who know where the edges of a bed are. The room narrows to the heat where skin meets skin; the fire throws a warm coin at our feet; the old boards under the rug keep the secret. When I slide my hand to the small of her back—the place my hand has learned like a name—her breath catches on a laugh, then rides back as a gasp that makes my body choose speed and then be told easy by the palm she sets on my jaw. I obey. Of course I do. I was made to.

"I want to watch," I manage, voice gone to gravel. "Let it take."

She does—eyes open, on me—until the seeing undoes her and she tips her head back and the ceiling gets to witness the kind of truth you can't write down without the room signing it. I follow close behind, not because I can't help it, but because I choose to, and the choice puts a rightness under it that scrubs me clean.

We breathe like we earned it.

Thunder rolls the long way down the glen. The ember in the grate rounds itself into a daft wee heart and holds. We lie there grinning like thieves and saints who got away with it.

"Tea," I say into her hair, because the human body is a small animal that likes a biscuit.

"Bring the whole kettle," she sighs, shameless and proud, and I am, indescribably, a man who deserves hot water and laughter with a woman sprawled across his chest like a claim.

I do bring the kettle. And the heel of the honey loaf. She eats with her knees up under the quilt and calls me carpenter in a tone the kirk ladies would find educational. We drink between kisses that are less intent now and more like congratulations. The storm tries one last, artful run at the roof; the cabin shrugs. We are warm enough to forgive weather for being weather.

When the mugs are empty and the candle is halfway down, she gets that look she gets—the one that says I am going to ask for something and you can say no but you won't. It is a good look. It sets my pulse under her hand to a more interesting tempo.

"Teach me," she says, wicked and shy in the same breath. "Not chisels. Not yet. Your other craft. The slow one."

I know what she means. The way I set a pace and keep it. The way I temper want with choice until the edge is right. I put my palm at her hip and feel the bone under my hand and the heat above it and the trust that sits between like the best kind of weight. "Aye," I say, and mean to be worthy of the ask. "We'll mind the fire."

We re-enter the weather by a different door.

I show her how small things change big ones: the place a thumb sits; the angle of a wrist; the power in stillness that isn't denial but attention given form. We talk more this time, patient and outrageous, truths and jokes braided until the line hums. She's quick, stubborn, shameless—an engineer taking a new machine apart with her hands and grinning when it purrs. She asks for what she wants with both language and body; I give it back and ask again because reciprocity is the only spell I believe in.

The second crest is quieter, deeper—the kind that makes time lose its corners. When it takes her, she says aye like she's signing a paper and then laughs on the way down and drags me with her, generous to the last. I swear I feel the beam approve. The fox absolutely does.

After, we lie crosswise under the quilt like a quotation mark and its answer. The window has written our breath and wiped it away twice; the wind is a tired uncle in the chair. Her fingertips draw a nonsense path on my forearm—loops, ladders, the plan of a house we haven't built yet and already live in. I put my hand at her nape and keep it there because she asked me not to leash myself and I'm learning how to carry heat without dropping my name.

"Tell me something true," she says, not because she needs proof, but because we like the sound of it in this room.

I look at the plane on the bench, at the ash shavings still curled like pale macaroni in the tray, at the oak slab behind the barn with the curl like a river under ice. "I thought I'd run out of firsts," I say. "Tonight proved me wrong."

Her mouth tips into a smile I'll spend the rest of my life earning. "My turn," she says, and kisses my sternum because apparently, she decided I'd like to be unmade every ten minutes. "I used to be afraid that want would make me small. With you, it makes me...more."

The right answer is gratitude. I make a quieter sound and hold her, because other words have to be earned and I've spent most of mine tonight.

The storm tires. The rafters take a last stretch. The candle gutter-kisses the rim and steadies. We drift toward sleep slow, like a boat easing into a berth. I keep my palm at her back and feel the steady lift of breath. She has both hands in my hair because she likes the way it steadies me. Balance. Bread and fences. Want and yes.

Somewhere between waking and the good dark I remember the ceilidh and the hay-bale geometry that will save shins, and I hear Hamish calling me a numpty for something I haven't done yet, and I smile into her hair for the sheer rightness of being a man in a warm room with a woman who laughs when the roof makes weather and writes on my arm like I'm a ledger worth the ink.

"Tomorrow we dance," I murmur.

"In time," she answers, already half under, and then, softer, "Mo chridhe."

"Aye," I say to the ceiling and the fox and the ember heart. "Aye."

Outside, the wind signs its name on the last of the night and leaves the page. Inside, the pumpkins keep their coins lit to morning, guarding the blue door like they know what lives behind it.

Chapter 19 — The Long Flame

Samantha's POV

Glenkeld strings the night like a fiddle.

Lanterns bloom along the green, hay bales shoulder-to-shoulder in a ring we helped lay yesterday, the band tuning until the air itself hums. Children hare past with turnip lanterns held high like saints who forgot to be solemn. The sky is a blue bruise fading to black; frost thinks about it and decides to wait. My scarf is his, my mouth is still his from last night, and the fox on my blue door winked—not literal—close enough when I left as if he'd been invited to the ceilidh and planned to cut in.

Ethan finds me at the edge of the crowd the way he always does now—like a compass acknowledging north. Clean flannel, hair obeying no one, that slow, wrecking smile that lands where my ribs meet. He offers his hand without theatrics. I put mine in it as if I've been doing nothing else all my life.

"Near?" he asks.

"Closer," I answer, and the band launches as if they heard.

We dance. God help us, we dance. He minds my steps like he promised—hand warm and steady at the small of my back, a quiet pressure that says here, now, together. When I trip on the turn after Katie's elbow finds me, he catches me with a small, sure lift that feels like a sentence finished. Hamish whoops like a gull with opinions and Mrs. Baxter pretends not to smile, then does anyway. Heat builds not from the hearth but from us—every spin a yes, every catch a promise.

Between reels we walk the ring with steaming cups pressed to our palms, breath ghosting, the wind nosing at us like a curious bairn. Ethan's knuckles brush mine, then stay. We don't look at our hands. We don't need to. The pumpkins lined along the bales glow like coins paid into a common pot; the bonfire at the far end throws sparks that take one look at the sky and decide to be stars instead.

"Tell me something true," I say, tucked into his side, my cheek in the hollow below his shoulder.

He doesn't reach for pretty. "I am happy enough I'm a little afraid," he says simply. "And I mean to keep it by choosing it."

The band drags us back before I can speak. We reel again, then a slow set that nudges strangers close until they aren't. I fit into him in the simple ways—palm to palm, foot to foot—and in the ways that live under my sternum: steadied, seen, chosen. When the tune drops to a hush, the whole town breathes with it, as if the green itself has a chest. The last note lands. Applause shakes the ribbons strung between posts. In the window of the smithy, a carved fox shadow laughs and refuses to apologise—not literal—close enough.

"I'm taking you home," Ethan says, low, like an oath softened by honey. Not a question. Not a claim. A plan we made together.

"Aye," I say, and something inside me that's been braced since cities and old names relaxes its grip.

We peel off before Hamish can smuggle us into another set. The night is crisp enough to bite; our breath plumes. Glenkeld quiets one lane at a time, doors closing with that contented sound only towns with good bones make. At Rowan Lane, my pumpkins are waiting—his lopsided grin and my clean glow, the two lights making a pill of gold—twin light making one pool—where our boots stop.

He pauses, fingers grazing the frame as he always does, communion with wood and hinge and the word home. "Yours?" he asks, eyes on the blue door. Or ours, the question really is. I hear it.

"Tonight," I say, unlocking. "Ours."

Inside, the cottage gathers us with warm breath. I set the latch. He sets his lantern down and every candle nudges higher with a soft whoomph—not literal—close enough, as if showing off. The fox knocker—brazen thing—throws one last shadow across the rug and settles to gossip with the letter slot.

We don't rush. We're past rushing. We're also past pretending we don't know what's coming, as if the town itself hasn't been steering us to this: bread and fences and storms and dances and the good drag of yes. He shrugs out of his flannel; I tug the ribbon loose from my hair. The room murmurs approval in small ways—the kettle's gentle click, the hearth's soft whoomph as it remembers heat. My heart thuds against my ribs like it's been allowed back into the house.

Autumn in Glenkeld: Pumpkins & Firelight

"Deliberate?" he says, last benediction, eyes on my mouth.

"Deliberate," I say, and close the inch.

The kiss is not gentle. It's not unkind, either. It's the kind you give when you've mapped the room, checked the hinges, and mean to live here: thorough, hungry, true. He tastes like cider and peat and the relief of being chosen in public and in private. When his hand finds the usual place at my back and fits, something in me drops its weapon and walks toward the fire.

"Say when," he breathes, and it isn't rote now; it's ritual.

"Not yet," I return, and add, bold with a woman's right, "Soon. Don't make me beg."

His laugh is brief and grateful and not at all gentlemanly. "Aye, sunshine."

We walk each other backwards and forget who's leading. The table knocks my hip (fondly); the quilt remembers last night and volunteers; the hearth throws coins up our calves. He unthreads my dress like he's been learning the knot all week and leaning on patience; I unbutton his shirt like it's a chisel box, careful and greedy. Cloth slides. Skin says yes without looking for permission. The air between us tightens until it hums like a tuned string.

And then—God—heat.

Not frantic. Not tidy. The long flame. His hands are everywhere and never hurried, a man who minds the fire and knows what good wood can do. I am shameless and soft in my asking. We meet in the middle of the rug as if there were always a mark chalked there with our names. The pumpkins throw their light through the window and spill it on the floorboards, striping us in gold and shadow. The fox turns his head in the glass as if he can't help himself.

"Mo chridhe," Ethan says into the place beneath my ear, the Gaelic made of iron and velvet both.

"Again," I ask, wrecked. "And—please."

He does, and then—because he knows how to wield yes like a tool—he asks me with his mouth and his hands and the whole of his careful body if I mean the next inch, and the next, and the one after. I say yes until the word goes quiet and becomes light.

The world compresses to heat and breath and the rhythm that finds us as if it's been waiting in the boards. He holds me like he means fully—not just arms and hips and breath, but the steadiness under all of it, the choosing. There is a moment where my old body wants to pull back, trained by thin love and loud rooms; he feels it before I do, lifts his head, and the question in his eyes is not doubt.

"Here?" he asks. Still sure? Still ours?

"Here," I say, and the yes opens like a door hung true.

He answers with something I have no words for. It isn't show. It isn't gentling for pity or grabbing for proof. It's...claiming, but only because I claimed him first and we built a place where claiming isn't taking, it's keeping. He moves like a man who trusts his hands and sets the pace like he promised, slow until it isn't, then slower again at the edge that asks for it. When I arch, he steadies. When I laugh—

because joy isn't polite—he grins against my mouth and makes it worse, better. When I want more, I say more, and there is more.

The room joins in with its ridiculous magic. The candle flame on the table lifts into a perfect wee heart and holds—not literal—close enough. The ember in the grate rounds itself as if pleased to be on theme—not literal—close enough. A draft worries the ribbon on the chair and then gives up, deciding it can't compete.

"Look at me," he says, right at the point where names stop being nouns, and I do, and the seeing does it—I tip cleanly over, like a leaf letting go at last in a good wind. Heat cracks into bright; my mouth finds his name as if it's a rope, and he follows a heartbeat after, strong and relieved, like a door set into place and tested and found worthy.

We breathe like the room earned it.

There's an aftermath I didn't know to want: the way his weight settles without pinning, the way my body stays mine and also his because we decided it, the way the town outside seems to hush out of courtesy. My cheek is damp with tears I didn't feel begin; he thumbs them away like a careful man sanding the last rough edge off a good piece.

"Still with me?" he asks, voice hoarse and sweet.

"Aye," I say, and laugh because the word feels enormous in my mouth and exactly right. "All the way in."

We don't hurry back to upright. The long flame is not done with us—it stretches, it purrs, it asks for a slower second that feels like rebuilding right there on the rug: the same shape, the new steadiness. We give it what we can. He tips into me with a care that makes my throat ache. I meet him with my whole, unruly heart. It doesn't look tidy from the ceiling. It looks like two people who chose the same weather.

After, the ordinary returns as a blessing. I fetch the kettle in a robe that does nothing to keep his eyes gentlemanly and is thanked for it. He brings the quilt up over my knees and steals my cup and then returns it and apologises with his mouth. We eat two of Katie's extra knots with our fingers and our good sense. He licks sugar from my wrist because he's a menace and I tell him to do it again because I am. The fox in the window fog sneaks us a grin and we allow it, because we won.

"Tell me something true," I say, curled into him on the sofa, his palm a steady weight at my hip, the kind of touch that admits to history and plans.

He thinks, eyes open—no hiding, never. "I used to brace for the after," he says. "Wait for the crack. I'm not bracing." His thumb draws a circle I feel in muscle and marrow. "If the wind comes up, we'll nail the shutter and set another log."

I tuck my nose into his shoulder to keep from spilling over again. "My turn," I say, finding the corner of his mouth, kissing it lightly because deeper would be reckless and right and we've already been both. "I'm not small. Not with you. I'm not loud, either. I'm…exact."

He makes a sound that says he's storing the word where he keeps good tools.

We tidy the room that isn't untidy, the way people do who worship at practical altars. He straightens the candle, sets the poker so no one trips. I rinse cups. The pumpkins on the step burn down a notch, patient as old dogs. The lane beyond the curtain shines a little with a frost that decided to go easy.

In bed, under the tartan, we don't reach for heat again. We hold it. He tucks me under his chin; I draw a nonsense map on his forearm in the dark—loop to loop, a floor plan for a table not yet built and already beloved. He answers with his palm at my back, the shape of permission and the weight of keeping.

"Tomorrow," he says, voice gone to the soft burr that only shows up when the room is safe. "We'll fetch the oak slab. You can see the curl in daylight."

"Tomorrow," I say. "We'll set the pumpkins out early. We'll mind the fire."

"Aye."

The cottage ticks its small contentment. Outside, a fox barks once, neat as a nail tapped home. The ember in the grate remains itself and, for a heartbeat, the heart-shape again—as if the room couldn't help it.

—not literal—close enough.

I sleep, not like a woman who fell. Like a woman who was caught and put down where she said.

Chapter 20 — Ever After, Kept Warm

Ethan's POV

Dawn comes in on quiet feet, the kind of light that doesn't boast—just lays a hand on the sill and waits to be noticed. The hearth has dossed down to a glow. The pumpkins on her—our—step are still shouldering out a last amber coin or two, as if they refused to sleep on the job. The room smells of peat and sugar and that clean, impossible note that's only her.

We are a tangle under the tartan. Not wrecked—remade. Her breath moves easy against my chest; my palm sits at the small of her back because it's learned the road and refuses to go anywhere else. She shifts in the soft way people do when they're already safe and wakes with a wee hum that puts a long, foolish smile on my face before I can stop it.

"Morning," she says, voice gone to velvet.

"Morning, sunshine."

We don't hurry. We let the light take its time measuring the beams. We listen to the cottage make its pleased ticks and sighs. When she tips her face up, there's a question in it that isn't really a question. I answer with my mouth, soft and sure—the kind of kiss that holds instead of takes. The kind that knows the house and is minded to keep it.

"Deliberate?" she whispers against my lip.

"Aye."

We make a small, slow ceremony of it—foreheads resting, laughter quick on the edge, hands that know the map now and enjoy tracing it again as if for the first time. No hurry. No proving. Just the long, steady heat of yes put to good use. When the ember in the grate rounds itself into that daft wee heart for a bare breath and then settles—not literal—close enough—I don't say anything. I don't have to. The room knows us; we know the room.

Tea after, because the human body is a small animal that likes ritual. Toast, a scandal of butter, honey that tastes like heather and summer saved in a jar. She eats perched on the counter in my shirt; I pretend it's a safety risk so I can touch her knee. The fox knocker on the blue door throws a shadow across the rug like a signature and, I swear, behaves itself for an entire minute. The candle on the table lifts its flame twice with a soft whoomph—not literal—close enough, then goes back to manners.

"Tell me the plan," she says, eyes bright, hands wrapped round her mug.

"Plan is—" I set the kettle back on for one more round because optimism is its own spice—"we carry the oak slab into the shop and you help me mark where the curl wants the legs. Then we'll set it on trestles and pretend it's a table already. Then we'll walk to the square because if we don't absorb praise from five separate retirees about our dancing, they'll feel robbed."

She grins, dangerous and dear. "And after the retirees?"

"After," I say, finding the nerve that's been walking the house all night, "we put the first two bowls on that table and call it ours."

Ours lands like a plank set true. She doesn't flinch. She doesn't joke it away. She reaches without ceremony, takes my hand, and turns it to kiss the inside of my wrist where pulse lives.

"Aye," she says simply. "Ours."

The yard smells like frost reconsidering itself. I lift the tarpaulin on the stack and the slab shows its face: pippy oak with a ribbon of curl running its heart, figure waking as soon as the light tests it. She inhales like a lass meeting a comet. I angle the lamp; the grain moves under the surface—cat's paw, river riffle, the kind of shimmer you get when a tree fought the wind and won.

"It breathes," she says, laying her palm flat. The wee hairs along my arm sit up as if the board spoke aye and meant it.

"Trees keep a ledger," I remind her, because she likes truth said plain. "Every ring a story. Cut honest and the story shows."

"We'll cut honest," she says, and it feels like we're talking about more than wood.

We haul it together steady, laughing, that peculiar satisfaction that comes from carrying the same weight. In the shop, I chalk a line where the legs will want to go; she leans in, precise as an engineer and twice as bold. When she draws a shy curve to follow the curl, the shavings we lift off the edge with a block plane curl like ribbons and drop onto her wrist, warm as breath. She laughs under it, and the sound makes the rafters move their shoulders like men at the back of a church pretending they feel nothing.

"Here," I say, stepping behind her, hands over her hands on the plane. One pass. Two. The ash tray fills with pale spirals like snow that forgot to be cold.

"It sings," she says, hushed and fierce all at once.

"Aye."

I set the slab on trestles and it looks like a promise. Then I fetch the wee thing I shouldn't have made yet and made anyway: a shallow drawer, dovetailed true, with a brass fox inlaid on the pull because I am predictable and we need a witness with a sense of humour. Inside, nestled on a square of tartan, there's a key to my door tied with a sliver of rowan-red ribbon and a brass washer she pressed into my palm last week for luck—punched and polished now, engraved on one side with a curl-line that matches the slab and on the other with aye.

I don't make a speech. I'm not Hamish. I set the drawer on the slab and open it like a man who knows he's got a good piece and hopes the client agrees.

She looks. She goes very still. Then she lifts the key and the washer together like a person who understands talismans and engineering both. "Name it and it's twice true," she says, water bright in her eyes and a grin she could use to light the lane. "Ethan?"

"Aye." I clear my throat because my voice has decided to remember it's mortal. "Stay, if you want. Not all at once—

some mornings yours, some mine, some wherever the wind puts us. But let's build the table in the same room and stop pretending the rooms are different."

She slides the key onto the ribbon, ties the washer to it like a charm, and tucks the whole lot under her shirt to lie against her skin. When she looks up, it's with the sort of joy a man doesn't get to see twice. "I'm going to make you breakfast in pyjamas you will hate," she says, which is a yes in her language and mine. "And I'll bring my machine. And my spare slippers. And a fox sticker for that drawer you're pretending is for pencils."

"It's for secrets," I say, ruined. "And fox stickers, aye."

We stand a breath in the good quiet that follows a right choice. The air changes temperature. The fox on the mantel in the front room throws a shadow across the shop's threshold as if he's got a longer reach today—not literal—close enough.

"Come see the magic," she says suddenly, mischief and certainty braided in her mouth.

We step back into the lane. The smirr has burned off. The bunting leaves are bright as coins. She opens her palm under the eaves where our two pumpkins sit, and the little breeze that lives in the close curls itself into a ring I've never seen it manage before and sets a tiny spiral of leaves walking right between the carved faces, turning once, twice, as if to tip its hat. The candle stubs inside both pumpkins—burnt near out, mind you—lift small flames with a soft whoomph, like lads remembering their manners. A fox barks up on the brae, neat as a nail tapped home. The lamplight on Rowan Lane goes warm.

"Not magic," she says, a warning and a dare.

"Or maybe that," I answer, because a man can learn.

We walk hand in hand to the square because the town has questions it would like answered by the evidence of two mouths and four boots. There's soup and ribbing and Hamish describing our reel like a bard gone to seed; Mrs. Baxter pronounces our posture acceptable and our fencing excellent; Morag hands us a paper bag with scandal in it and tells us to behave later or at least to lock the door. Katie slips rosemary into Samantha's pocket and doesn't say why; she doesn't need to.

"Happy?" Hamish asks me, sly, hands in pockets, pretending he isn't checking the set of my shoulders the way brothers do.

I consider the blue door, the new table, the key tucked under a shirt I intend to find again before the kettle boils tonight. I consider the way she stands into weather. I consider the long flame that won't go out as long as we feed it measured and true.

"Aye," I say, simple and exact. "Enough to be careful with it."

He claps my shoulder hard enough to jar a tooth. "Numpty," he says, fond as bread.

— — —

Afternoon slips to the kind of gold that makes a man forgive previous weather. We carry the slab inside, set the drawer, set two bowls, two spoons, nothing showy. She brings her machine, sets it on the shelf like it's always lived there. I tuck a blanket in the basket by the hearth and pretend it was always for two. We stand in the doorway between rooms—the shop that smells of ash and oil and the cottage that smells of soup and beeswax—and it feels like a hinge swung easy on pins I set years ago not knowing what door they were for.

"Tell me something true," she says, fingertips in my back pocket like she owns the place and the pockets and the man.

"I will love you like a house," I say. Honest and plain. "I'll mend. I'll shore. I'll open windows when the room's gone stale and I'll shut them when the wind's a liar. I'll put the kettle on before you know you're cold."

She's quiet in that way that means I heard you; I'll keep it. Then, with that clarity of hers: "I will love you like a codebase," she says. "I'll refactor bad patterns. I'll write tests for the edge-cases. I'll name things clearly so we can find them later. And I'll ship joy, on purpose."

We are a pair of fools and the luckiest people I know.

Evening comes soft. We set the pumpkins out early. We light them together. Our two circles meet on the stone and make one long pill of gold—twin light making one pool—the way they always do, and I pretend to be surprised so I can watch her grin. The fox knocker—indefensible—winks like he wrote the day's script. In the grate, the ember lifts into a tiny heart and then a steadier glow, as if to say enough with the spectacle; keep me fed.

We will.

Inside, we christen the table with bowls and spoon-clatter and a loaf that thinks itself superior to butter and is wrong. We do the scandal Morag expected and also the washing up. The cottage ticks, pleased with itself. The blue door looks like a sky we've decided to keep.

Later, under the tartan, in the small hour when even the geese go quiet, she draws a nonsense plan on my forearm in the dark—loop, ladder, door. I lay my palm at her back the way I always mean to and always will.

"Happy ever after?" she says, too wry to say it straight, too brave to hide the hope.

"Not a spell," I answer, because truth sits best warm. "A practice." I kiss her hair. "We'll keep choosing. We'll mind the fire."

"Aye," she says into my throat, and the last of the pumpkins outside holds its wee glow to morning as if agreeing to take the first watch.

The fox barks once on the hill, neat as a nail tapped home—not literal—close enough.

✉ A Note from the Author

Thank you for coorie-ing in with me and spending time in Glenkeld. Writing this story has been like wrapping myself in a tartan blanket on a crisp autumn night — and I hope it brought you the same warmth and comfort.

The Glenkeld series will follow the seasons, each one with its own door to open and love story to tell. I'd love for you to come back as the leaves fall, the snow drifts, and the blossoms bloom.

Until then, may your nights be filled with pumpkins, firelight, and someone to coorie close to.

With love,
Kara S. Lang

🏴 A Wee Glenkeld Glossary

Coorie *(Scottish)* – To snuggle in, nestle close, or seek warmth and comfort. The perfect word for a cosy night by the fire.

Ceilidh *(pron. kay-lee)* – A traditional Scottish gathering with music, dancing, and storytelling. Expect laughter, reels, and maybe a wee dram.

Dreich *(dreekh)* – A wonderfully Scottish word for a grey, damp, miserable day. The kind that makes a fire, a book, and a blanket all the more inviting.

Blether – A friendly chat or gossip. In Glenkeld, you can't go to the shop without a good blether!

Clishmaclaver – Idle talk or chatter, often light-hearted.

Braw – Beautiful, fine, or excellent. A braw autumn sunset is something to behold.

Wee – Small, but used affectionately. In Glenkeld, everything good seems to start with "a wee…" — a wee dram, a wee hug, a wee romance.

Bairn – A child. A term of endearment often used in families.

Mo chridhe *(Gaelic)* – Pronounced *mo cree-ah*; literally "my heart." A deeply tender term of endearment for someone you love.

About the Series

Love the Highlands in autumn? Winter is coming to Glenkeld...

❄ Winter in Glenkeld: Snowflakes & Candlelight — coming soon!

A story of frosty nights, candlelit windows, and a romance that burns brighter than the cold.

About the Author

Kara S. Lang writes cosy, heartwarming romances set in the Scotland. Her Glenkeld series follows the seasons of a small village where every door hides a love story and every night is a chance to coorie in. When she's not writing, Kara can usually be found with a mug of something warm, wandering through the countryside that inspires her books.

Printed in Dunstable, United Kingdom